SEVEN THINGS NOT TO DO WHEN EVERYONE'S TRYING TO KILL YOU

THE TALE OF BRYANT ADAMS, BOOK TWO

MEGAN O'RUSSELL

D1603292

Ink Worlds Press

Visit our website at www.MeganORussell.com

Seven Things Not to Do When Everyone's Trying to Kill You

Copyright © 2019, Megan O'Russell

Cover Art by Sleepy Fox Studio (https://www.sleepyfoxstudio.net/)

Editing by Christopher Russell

Interior Design by Christopher Russell

Printed in the United States of America

DEDICATION

To the many Fairy Godmothers who have helped keep me alive along the way

SEVEN THINGS NOT TO DO WHEN EVERYONE'S TRYING TO KILL YOU

1

The monster dodged around the people of New York, daring to run within inches of the unsuspecting humans before darting down another path. But the tourists of Central Park were oblivious to the imminent danger charging toward them. Unaware that at any moment a magical creature could attack. Only one wizard was brave enough to hunt the beast. Only one wizard had the heart to defend the good people of New York.

"There!" Devon shouted, yanking me out of my inner monologue. "He's over there."

I bent double, squinting between the legs of the horde of tourists who crowded the Central Park paths. A streak of brown fur skidded across the frozen ground and off through the trees.

"Dammit." I pushed my way through the crowd. "Why is it still running?"

"Just come on!" Devon sprinted ahead of me, chasing the beast.

My lungs ached as I dodged people and trees, barely keeping the thing's tail in view. Buildings cut through the grass, blocking the creature's path. Soon we would have it pinned.

"Where does it think it's going?" Devon puffed. It was nice to know the last hour of running through the park had actually winded him.

A guttural roar split the air, and my heart sank as I recognized the brick buildings in front of us.

Of course the thing was running straight for the Central Park Zoo.

"We can't let it get in there!" I ran as fast as my exhausted, scrawny legs could muster. If that thing got into the zoo, there would be too many places for it to hide. Too many cages for us to search. If a zookeeper found it, it would make their career and headline news. And really ruin my week.

The creature dashed through a clearing in the trees as he made his final sprint for the zoo buildings.

"*Stasio!*" I shouted, my eyes fixed on the blur of brown fur. The air surrounding the thing shimmered for a moment before the creature smacked into the brand new solid box my spell had formed around it.

"Nice one, Bry," Devon panted, his hands on his knees as he stopped next to the creature.

"Thanks." I don't mean to sound like a prick, but I really was pretty proud of myself. A perfect, crystal-clear square, like Snow White's glass casket, sealed in the angry critter. "For a little guy, he's freakin' fast."

The fur ball squeaked and clawed against the spell like he had heard my words and found the word *little* to be insulting.

"He really doesn't look so bad." I knelt, letting the chill of the frozen ground drain the heat of the run from me.

"Doesn't look so bad?" Devon rubbed his gloved hands over his face. "How often do you see a two-headed squirrel the size of a house cat with a bright green lizard tail running through Central Park?"

Devon's description was on the whole completely accurate.

Though the squirrel was a little smaller than my mom's cat, it did have two heads, both of which swiveled to glare at me. One had black eyes, the other creepy red. I shuddered as they simultaneously started chirping at me. The forked lizard tail curled up over its head like a scorpion ready to strike.

"Okay, so it's a little creepy. *Conorvo.*" The squirrel's makeshift cage shrank, stopping just short of squishing the little guy.

"What I want to know is how no one noticed him," Devon said as I shrugged out of my bright red backpack. "A weird little nut-hunting baby dragon running around New York for two months and no one said anything? How is that even possible?"

Nutty McDragon, because the little dude deserved a name, squealed as I slid him into my backpack and closed the zipper.

"Really?" I hoisted myself to my feet, legs shaky after having run so far. "After everything that's happened, you think people pretending not to notice a weird squirrel in Central Park is strange?" I pointed to the sky west of us where a giant blue flower cut through the trees of Central Park, and then to the south where a stone tower loomed over Times Square.

"Okay, okay"—Devon raised his hands in surrender—"but still, people, man."

"People." I sighed and followed Devon back toward the path.

Nutty McDragon squealed like a mutant demon in my backpack, but other than a few people looking nervously at their phones, no one seemed to care as we made our way west.

Part of me wanted to be disappointed in humanity for not caring about weird squirrels, giant flowers, and stone towers of doom appearing in Manhattan, but since I was the one who had caused all three of them, I couldn't be too mad.

See, I'm a wizard. A super new wizard. Once upon a time, about two months ago, I had four really bad days. I found a phone that holds an illegal magical library, destroyed both my parents' homes, defeated an evil wizard, pissed off some other crazy powerful people, and almost died a couple of times. Not to mention the, you know, obvious magical damage to Manhattan. But I came out on the other side alive, a wizard, and with a girlfriend who embodies all things wonderful in the world, so really the hell days were worth it in the end.

We walked past the chain-link fence that surrounded the base of Big Blue, protecting the giant flower from protestors and wannabe flower killers. Scientists were researching the flower as a genetic anomaly. On the other side of the crisscrosses in the fence, they circled Big Blue's base like they did every day. Doing all sorts of sciencey things. I could make someone's career by giving them Nutty McDragon, but I didn't need another disaster on my head.

"Winter is here!" a protestor screamed as we passed. "It's time for the plant to die!"

"Wow," Devon muttered. "Do they have nothing else to do with their time?"

There were at least twenty people protesting around this side of Big Blue. And I had to give it to them—it was a little weird that, while the rest of the park had succumbed to the December freeze, Big Blue had stayed just as...blue. But the sign that read *The Aliens are breeding, destroy their nest now!* was way off. Aliens didn't make the giant bloom. I did. I blushed and ducked my head as we passed the alien protestor, like he might be able to read my mind or something.

I'd seen news stories about protestors surrounding the Times Square spire, too—some claiming demons from the underworld, others angry about sinking real estate prices with the new massive mineral neighbor. I had been upholding my New Yorker obligation and avoiding Times Square lately, so I didn't really know how weird those protestors were. Only that they were there every day and really pissed about my accidental architectural addition.

"Let Eric know we're on our way," Devon said when we reached the far west side of the park.

I pulled my phone from my pocket, checking to make sure I had the right, non-magical phone before pressing my finger to the scanner and dialing Eric.

"Did you finally manage it?" Eric drawled in a bored tone.

"Hello to you, too," I said. "And yes I—"

"We," Devon cut in.

"—*we* got it. I'm taking him to my mom's."

"Delightful." I could almost hear Eric's eye roll through the phone. "I'll meet you there."

I hung up and slid the phone back into my pocket.

"Is your mom going to be okay with Eric and Nutty being at the apartment?" Devon's eyebrows scrunched together. A pack of girls in chic winter coats passed, and his face immediately smoothed into racially ambiguous perfection. The girls giggled and waved as they passed. Nutty McDragon squealed his displeasure at the noise.

"Mom'll be fine with it." It wasn't true. I knew it wasn't true. Even Nutty, who was squirming around in my backpack more than any magically-contained creature should be able to, knew it wasn't true. But I didn't really have another choice, so we kept walking to my mom's, Devon winking at every remotely attractive woman, me trying to look inconspicuous with my shrieking backpack.

"You got a sewer rat in there?" An old black lady eyed my bag as we waited for a crosswalk.

"No ma'am, just trying to get his cat back from the vet," Devon said calmly as I opened my mouth to say...I don't know what. "The carrier broke, and it was the best we could do."

"It doesn't sound like any cat I've ever heard." The woman

shook her head. "You better be careful playing with angry animals. Some bites don't heal too well."

"We'll be careful."

The woman *tshed* her disbelief at our promise and waddled down the street, shaking her head.

Devon grabbed my elbow and steered me away. My feet wanted to carry me south to my mom's old house, but seeing as that one had been mostly destroyed, we turned north instead.

The doorman didn't look up from the dinging video game in his hands as we walked to the elevator.

"What service," Devon whispered sarcastically.

We lived on the twelfth floor of this building, and the elevator protested the whole way up. It wasn't a great place, but it was what my mom could afford. My dad offered to buy us an apartment—he was already looking for a new place himself, so he had a real estate dude and everything—but my mom wanted nothing to do with it. The concept of taking help, let alone money, from my dad was enough to turn even Mom's best moods sour. So we ended up in a place with chipped linoleum floors that smelled vaguely of nursing home.

Voices carried through the door before we reached it.

"I don't even want to know what you're bringing in here," Mom growled as I slipped the key into the lock. "What are you bringing into my home?"

"Seeing as you've just contradicted yourself," Eric said, "I'm not really sure how to answer you, Ms. Miller."

"Hey, Mom," I said, cutting her off as I opened the door. "How are you?"

"It depends on why Mr. Deldridge"—Mom growled his name—"is here."

On cue, Nutty McDragon started squealing. The squirrel knew just how to get me in trouble.

"Oh good God." Mom sank into a chair as Mrs. Mops, our

shaggy, gray, obese cat, leapt up onto the table by the door to bat at my bag.

"We found the squirrel," I said lamely, smiling to soften the blow.

"It only took you a week." Eric held out his hands for my backpack.

"But we found it." Devon flopped down onto the couch. "Had to run all over Central Park, mind you."

"One down, two to go." Eric pulled the shimmering cage that held Nutty McDragon from my bag. "At least we hope only two."

"Just try for optimism." Devon sighed and closed his eyes.

"I'm sorry," I said for the millionth time. You see, the same day I accidentally made Big Blue, I did another spell. One I thought hadn't worked at all. Only it had. Little bits of magic drifted off into Central Park and did a minuscule amount of damage to a few of the resident animals. And by damage, I mean an extra head and lizard tail. At least for Nutty. We hadn't actually seen the other two animals.

"What in the hell are you going to do with it?" Mom leaned in to examine Nutty, her eyes narrowing as he chittered at her. "I will not have an animal exterminated in my home."

My mom would never kill a mouse or rat or anything in our apartment. I never pointed out the irony of letting Mrs. Mops do the killing for her. I just wanted the rodents dead, and if Mrs. Mops wanted to be a vermin serial killer, so be it.

"Can you make him a normal squirrel again?" I sank onto the couch next to Devon.

"It might be possible." Eric held Nutty up to the light. "But it would be difficult to remove the right head. I'm not entirely sure which holds most of the poor thing's brain."

"So, what are you going to do?" I asked over Mrs. Mop's growling as her paws slid uselessly down Nutty's cage.

"Rehome it." Eric shrugged. "I can take it to Beville. The

thing seems to have a reasonable temperament. There might be someone in need of a new pet."

"Would Lola want him?" I asked, thinking of her colorful home with lots of drapes to climb.

"Lola doesn't approve of rodents." Eric placed Nutty back into my backpack. "And I don't think Lola's guard would like him hanging around either. Don't worry, I'll find a home for him somewhere. You should concentrate on finding whatever other disasters you created."

"Any tips on how to start?" My feet throbbed at the very thought of tracking down the other two creatures I'd inadvertently created.

"The same I've given before. Track the magic in Central Park. If it's an animal that doesn't look right, catch it before we have any more magic making headline news." Eric strode to the door. "Call me when you've found something else."

And with that, Eric, Nutty, and my backpack were all gone.

"I really don't like that man." Mom got out the vacuum and started cleaning where Eric had stood. "I really, really don't like that man."

"I can meet him somewhere else." I spoke over the *whir* of the vacuum, hope rising a centimeter in my chest at the suggestion.

"You are not meeting him unsupervised," Mom half-shouted. "I may not be able to keep my son from being a wizard, but I will not have him fraternizing with criminals without supervision."

"Right." I didn't dare look at Devon. "You're totally right."

"Ms. Miller, is it okay if Bryant comes out with me tonight? I want to walk around, but it wouldn't be safe to go alone." Devon sounded disgustingly sincere, young, and hopeful.

"Of course, Devon." Mom nodded. "I think Bryant spending time with his *normal* friends is a great idea."

"Thanks, Ms. Miller." Devon and I both leapt to our feet.

My legs twinged in protest at being asked to move again. But sitting wasn't an option. We had places to be, and we still had our coats on and everything.

"Be back soon," I said as we walked into the corridor.

"You should invite Elizabeth," Mom called after us.

"Only your mother would worry more about you spending time with your mentor than your girlfriend," Eric said in a thoroughly bored and disdainful tone as he leaned next to our door, holding my red backpack.

My stomach did an Olympic gymnastics floor routine at the word *girlfriend.*

"Well, Elizabeth has never almost gotten all of us killed," Devon said as we headed down the hall.

Eric smiled. "Touché."

2

The steps down to the Columbus Circle subway station were crammed with people. New Yorkers looking harassed, tourists looking confused. A man with steel drums thumped out "O Christmas Tree" with a red-and-white top hat sitting in front of him for tips. The sun had started to set, and New York was ready for Christmas magic in a way only a city built on shining lights and commercialism could ever be.

"How long do you think we have?" Devon asked.

"Before my mom freaks out?" I asked, not wanting to voice the other options for answers to that question.

"If we make good time to Beville," Eric said, weaving through tourists with a vague look of disapproval on his face, "we should be able to get a full hour of training in and get you home before your mother begins to panic. It really would be much simpler if you could move to Beville, or at the very least were able to spend more than a few hours a week on your training."

"My mom can't know you're teaching me anything." I ducked under the flailing arms of a gaggle of girls trying to take a selfie. "If she knew, she'd want to be there, and then she'd know what we're doing, and then she could end up in a magical cocoon halfway to dead again."

"I totally agree we need to keep your mom as far away from magic as we can, Bry," Devon said as we made it inside the station. "But how long do you think she's going to buy you're only seeing Eric for critter capture reasons?"

"Listen to the boy, Bryant," Eric said. "I have a feeling Mr. Rhodes has spent a fair amount of time lying to ladies. He must be an expert by now."

"I resent that," Devon said as we passed the ticket machines.

A pack of tourists had lined up, trying to buy subway passes. The New Yorkers behind them looked like they might riot if the tourists couldn't figure out how to insert their credit cards stat.

"I may have worked my way through a fair number of women—"

"More like girls," I countered.

Devon ignored me "But I have never lied, cheated, or..."

They kept going, Devon prattling on about chivalry or something, Eric laughing snobbishly at him, both agreeing my mom would find out about my secret wizard training eventually. But their words got all muffled under the blissful humming in my ears as soon as I saw Elizabeth leaning against the subway platform wall.

She looked at me with her sparkly, perfect eyes, and her smile made my heart fly right out of my chest. Wind seemed to carry her gently toward me as her black and blonde-streaked hair floated around her shoulders.

Her fingers twined through mine, and she kissed me gently. As soon as our lips touched, my brain went even fuzzier, like I was living the happiest dream any human has ever had.

"We got one," Devon said, interrupting our moment and bringing me shattering back to Nutty McDragon-inhabited reality.

"Really?" Elizabeth turned to Devon but kept her hand firmly in mine.

"There are still two more to go." Eric led us down a side corridor. "And I doubt the next two will be as easy to catch."

"Thanks for that cheerful thought," I muttered.

Eric stopped in front of a blank stretch of wall, glanced around, then murmured. "*Portunda.*" With a tiny *crack* and a sprinkle of dust, a door appeared in the wall.

"Well, if you would help us, we could find them in a day and be done with it." Devon stepped through the newly created door.

"You and Bryant made the mistake—it is up to the two of you to fix it," Eric said.

My eyes swept the corridor. No one seemed to care that a door had appeared where it shouldn't have been. They were all too busy trying to avoid being pummeled by giant bags stuffed with Christmas gifts to spare us a glance.

Elizabeth pulled me gently through the door, and Eric shut it behind us. "*Portundo.* It's good for you to work on your own, and I have other things to be getting on with."

A knot settled in my stomach as we started down the long, sloping tunnel. Tiles mixed with the rough stone of the floor, and dim lights hung overhead. I knew the walk down to Beville well. It had become a sort of tri-weekly pilgrimage.

I could meet with Eric aboveground to chat about catching the unfortunate critters, or for coffee and tales about the history and hierarchy of magic, but for actual spell practice, we had to go belowground to Beville. Where all the wizards in New York lived and no one would get too mad if I accidentally caught something on fire while trying to levitate. Unless I caught a person on fire. That guy had gotten really, really mad.

"Speaking of other things for you to be getting on with,"

Devon said after we had been walking in silence for a few minutes, "any word on our impending doom?"

"Mr. Rhodes, have you learned nothing about discretion?" Eric sighed.

"Elizabeth, are there any creepy crawlies listening to us?" Devon stopped and turned toward Elizabeth.

She squinted into the dark corners of the tunnel, watching shadowy details I couldn't hope to see. "We're alone."

"It is useful having a seer around." Eric nodded.

"A baby seer," Elizabeth corrected.

"Still more skilled than the rest of us." Eric bowed. "There have been rumors of the Ladies. Activity in the Consortium and rumblings in the Library. The Consortium hasn't reopened for business yet, but we can assume it will quite soon. The residents of Beville are growing restless without the Library's resources. And without the Ladies' rule, others have tried to step into their place."

"On a scale of one to ten, how screwed are we?" Devon asked casually.

"I'd give us a seven." Eric turned and continued down the sloping tunnel. "We didn't destroy the Ladies in the Battle of Beville. Thaden did that."

My neck tensed at the name. It's hard to shake the bone-chilling fear of the guy who tried to kill you, even after he's dead.

"Though they might be a little testy about my slight rebellion," Eric said.

"A bit of an understatement, but sure," Elizabeth said.

"And allowing signs of magic to be seen aboveground is strictly forbidden."

"Sorry," I mumbled.

"Which is why it is of the utmost importance you catch the animals you altered. It is a show of good faith that you are trying to fix your mistakes."

"And you think Bryant catching the freaky squirrel is going to make the Ladies forget all the things they've tried to kill us for? Or now that most of them got slaughtered while they were trying to kill us, you think they'll just give it up as a bad job and leave us alone?" Devon said, fear barely audible beneath his cavalier tone.

"Of course they won't," Eric said. "They will blame us for the loss of their comrades and the disruption of order. But when they decide to come for us, I would like to have as much reason and justice on our side as possible."

"And when exactly do you think they might come?" Worry wiggled in my stomach.

"In a few years," Eric said as we entered the cavern.

My stomach stopped doing the terrified tango. In a few years, I might be competent enough to defend myself.

"Or they might come tomorrow while you're all clustered together at your lunch table," Eric said, bringing the dancing belly right back. "That's the trouble with having enemies who are powerful and slow to age. They lack the sense of urgency one requires when planning an appropriate defense."

We cut sideways around the giant column of stone that jutted up from the center of the street. Cracked and crumbling bits of rock littered the ground, but the stone spire itself was perfectly smooth as it rose from Beville to Times Square. I shuddered, remembering casting the spell that trapped Thaden in the stone, but Elizabeth, Devon, and Eric didn't spare the thing a glance. I guess they were used to it after having walked around it every time we went to Eric's house. And I suppose when you're in an underground city of magic there are better things to consider strange than a column of stone.

Rows of houses pressed up to the wide stone walls, which soared to the ceiling thirty feet overhead. Some of the houses looked like normal brownstones from the city above. Others...

not so much. One house had taken the shape of an enormous clock tower, and another tiny house perched high up in a tree. But we aimed for the gray stone house next to the white, clapboard Victorian.

The door to the house swung open as soon as Eric set foot on the stairs.

"Hello, old girl." Eric patted the doorjamb.

The floor of the house creaked as Eric stepped into the foyer, a low rumble that sounded almost like a cat purring filled the air.

"I'll see you in a bit." Elizabeth kissed my cheek and headed down the long hall toward the parlor where Eric kept his illegal collection of wizard-type books.

Devon and I followed Eric the other way, past the rows of shiny, locked, wooden doors, stopping at the very last door in the hall.

"You know, it really would be more useful if you went with Elizabeth and studied." Eric gave Devon a side-eyed glare as he opened the door to the training room. "You can observe Bryant learning magic as much as you like, but you will never be a wizard. Wizards are born, not created through observation."

"I like to think of myself as a chaperone." Devon grinned and pushed past Eric. "It's your job to train Bryant to survive the Ladies and whatever other shit your crazy magical mess can throw at him. It's my job to make sure *you* don't kill Bryant."

"Thanks, Devon." I punched him in the arm on my way to the center of the room.

I'd never say it out loud, but having Devon with me in training really did make our imminent death feel a little further away.

The training room had been a ballroom. Shining parquet floors sparkled under a giant crystal chandler. Wallpaper with gold inlay glistened above and below the intricately carved chair rail. Our footsteps echoed around the room that, by non-magic standards, was too large to fit in the house. A lot of the rooms in Eric's house were too large to fit in Eric's house. It always felt a little bit creepy, like I was standing in a place that wasn't meant to exist. But it was just another charming part of living with magic, accepting the impossible as a part of daily life.

"So what are we working on today?" I asked as I shrugged out of my coat and tossed it to Devon. "Lightning whips to bind attackers? Levitation to distract enemies? I made the cage work for Nutty."

"It is a pretty great cage," Devon said as Eric pulled Nutty out of my backpack.

"An excellent cage." Eric set Nutty on the ground. "*Vanexo.*" Nutty's shimmering cage disappeared. "But you need more of a challenge to be getting on with. *Libargo.*"

With a *screech*, Nutty grew, not stopping until he had reached the size of a Great Dane. Nutty thumped his arm-width tail happily on the ground, shaking the floor. The chandelier creaked in protest.

"Nutty," Eric said. Both of Nutty's heads swiveled to Eric. Light glinted off his black and red eyes. Eric smiled and pointed at me. "Attack."

"What the—" I didn't have time to finish swearing at Eric before Nutty launched himself at my face like he knew damn well I was responsible for his newfound two-headedness.

I opened my mouth to shout a spell, but couldn't think of a spell to shout that wouldn't hurt poor Nutty.

Nutty didn't care as much about hurting me. His claws dug into my shoulders, and his tail whacked me in the stomach, knocking the wind out of me. But his two mouths baring sharp teeth were the most terrifying.

"*Conorvo!*" I screamed the spell, but Nutty didn't shrink. I managed to get my bleeding arm under his stomach and toss him off me before he shredded my face. "*Primurgo!*" My shield shimmered into being around me.

Nutty threw himself at my shield, spitting and hissing.

"You cannot simply hide in a shield, Bryant." Eric rolled his eyes at me. "The point is for you to learn how to fight, not hide."

"Hiding sounds like a much better option!"

"You can do it, Bry," Devon cheered me on from his nice, safe, non-bleeding place by the door.

"You know what? Fine." I let go of the magic holding up my shield. "*Kunga.*" The spell whipped out and struck Nutty in the stomach like I'd sucker-punched him. He skidded across the glass-smooth floor, furry little butt over head. I didn't have time for the self-loathing at hitting an animal to set in before the demon had gotten back to his feet and charged, teeth gnashing.

"Oh, it's on."

3

"Ouch, ouch," I grunted with every step as I hobbled my way back out of the Columbus Circle subway station, wishing PETA would just come after me for battling an evil animal and put me out of my misery. "Ouch."

Elizabeth was kind enough not to laugh as she wrapped her arm around my waist to help me up the stairs. It was nearly ten, and the daytime crowds had cleared. It was nice not to be buffeted by people with every step, but it left more chances for people to notice me.

"You should just heal yourself, dude," Devon said in a stage whisper. "Eric told you to try it."

"Shh," Elizabeth warned as a man cut a wide arc on the stairs to avoid coming near me.

I didn't blame him. Dear sweet Nutty McDragon had left cuts on my cheek and arms with his claws and a nice bite on my right calf. My coat covered the blood on my arms, but not what leaked out of my face, and my pants were torn and gross.

"I was just saying he should." Devon shrugged.

"And risk healing my nose right off my face?" I whimpered as we made it to level ground, preparing myself for the rest of the torturous walk home.

"It could be a new fashion." Devon grinned.

"Really not helping, Dev." Elizabeth glared at him.

He shrunk a little under her sparkly glare. "I'm just gonna take the long way home." Devon stepped out of Elizabeth's reach, giving an Eric-like bow. "I'll see you at school tomorrow, oh wonderful squirrel tamer."

"Devon!" Before Elizabeth could shout anything else at him, he disappeared into a crowd of drunken tourists.

"It was a little funny," I said meekly.

"It's not funny at all." Elizabeth kept her arm around me even though we were walking on flat sidewalks. "Having your face scratched half off by a mutant rodent is not funny."

"A least it wasn't a mutant turtle," I muttered.

A tiny smile glimmered on her lips for a moment. "But what's your mom going to say? What are you going to tell her?"

"Bar fight?"

"It's not funny." Elizabeth stopped and stepped in front of me to look into my poop-brown eyes with her diamond ones. "Eric letting a monster maul you isn't funny. Hiding what we're doing isn't funny. I"—she ran her hands through her hair, mussing her multicolored curls in the most breathtaking way—"I know you need to train. I know you need to learn to fight. We all chose to be a part of Beville and magic and all of it. We all knew it wouldn't always be safe..."

"But?" I wrapped my arms around her waist. It still astounded me that she didn't tell me not to touch her. That she actually melted a little and drew herself closer to me.

"But," she began, tears glistening in the corners of her eyes, "if this is what a training session with a demonic squirrel—"

"A magically enhanced demonic squirrel."

"—leaves you looking like, what's going to happen when the

Ladies decide to come after us again?" Elizabeth pressed on. "Or when some of Thaden's creatures decide to crawl up from the shadows? Or some evil asshole decides to take Thaden's place?"

"We'll figure it out."

She pressed her forehead to mine.

Even in frozen Manhattan, where the scent of gas and garbage were the usual aromas, Elizabeth smelled like fresh spring flowers.

"I almost lost you once." Elizabeth brushed her lips against mine. "I don't want to do that again."

I smiled. I mean a broad, soul-glowing smile.

It might seem weird since Elizabeth was talking about the time I had nearly died. But having the most wonderful girl in the world look truly terrified at the prospect of losing you can sort of make your heart grow three sizes.

"If something happens again—"

"*When* it happens," Elizabeth said. "This is Eric we're talking about. Disaster is a *when* with Eric Deldridge as our fearless leader."

"*When* some new scary thing comes our way, we'll be better prepared." I brushed the tears from her cold cheek with my equally icy thumb. "We've been training hard. I actually under-stand a teeny tiny bit about how to use magic. When another monster or Lady or whatever comes after us, we'll be ready. I promise."

A gust of freezing wind whipped down the street. Elizabeth huddled her face into my coat as the sudden cold tore past us.

"We should get home." Elizabeth took my hand and pulled me down the street as soon as the wind stopped. "There must be a storm coming."

But the prickle on my neck didn't stop when the night went back to its normal level of unpleasant cold. The feeling of dread followed me the rest of the way home and settled itself into my stomach as I wondered if it had been meteorology or fate that blasted us on the sidewalk.

I didn't say anything to Elizabeth as we walked hunched against the cold, gripping hands and moving as quickly as my hobbled leg could carry me. We didn't stop until we reached the florescent-lit lobby of my building.

"Do you want me to come up?" Elizabeth asked.

It wasn't like a *Do you want me to come up* in a Hollywood movie kind of way. It was a *Hey, do you want me to come and lie to your mom for you since you're incapable of lying in a convincing manner* sort of thing.

"I don't know." I touched the squirrel cuts on my face.

"Dude," the desk guy said, inexplicably choosing this moment to actually care what was happening in the lobby, "you should put some cream on that."

"Right, cream. Thanks." Elizabeth took me by the elbow and led me to the elevator. "We'll just tell your mom Nutty broke out of his cage."

"Eric was supposed to have left the building without us." I leaned against the wall by the elevator door, trying not to wonder why it was making such a low grinding sound. "Was I mugged?"

"She'd want to file a police report." Elizabeth frowned. Lines appeared on her forehead. They were the cutest little lines I had ever seen.

"We could say I fell?"

"And got perfectly lined up cuts and a bite mark?"

"Pissed off a dog walker with an angry dog?"

"Do you want your mom to make you get rabies shots?" Elizabeth asked. She bit her lips together and glanced up and down the abandoned hallway. "I think you should try a healing spell. Eric wouldn't have told you to do it if he didn't think you could."

I swallowed a laugh.

"You can't just walk around like this. Those cuts could get infected," Elizabeth whispered. "He may be a lizard squirrel, but you were still bitten by a wild animal."

I opened my mouth to argue, found I didn't have an argument to make, and sighed. "Fine, but if I end up with no nose—"

"I won't dump you." Elizabeth kissed the tip of my nose. "Just in case I never see it again."

"Thanks." I pulled the black cell phone from my pocket. Even after everything that phone had been through, it still looked perfect. Not a crack in the glass, not a ding in the case. I pressed my thumb to the scanner, and the screen instantly blinked on.

I swiped over to the healing app—a shimmering drop of blood against a white background. The image didn't make me feel any better.

"Should we go into the elevator?" Elizabeth asked as the door dinged open.

I shook my head, scanning the spells in the app. If something went wrong, I definitely didn't want to be sans nose and trapped in the world's jankiest elevator.

Flesh wounds. The straightforward description seemed promising. Like the phone was finally trying to make one damned thing easy. Like it had tried to idiot proof magical healing.

I clicked on the underlined words.

Healing a flesh wound is a rudimentary skill. The incantation to be used is Sinato. *If, however, there is venom present in the wound, the venom must be treated before the skin can be healed. If the venom is healed into the skin, the venom will become integrated with the new flesh and impossible to remove. Death will be inevitable.*

"Inevitable death," I murmured. "Sounds great."

"Does Nutty have venom?" Elizabeth asked.

"I don't think so. I don't feel sick or tingly or anything." I mouthed *Sinato*, rolling it around in my mouth until it felt natural. "Here goes nothing." I glanced up and down the hall one more time before speaking. "*Sinato*."

The pain was instant. Like someone had poured boiling hydrogen peroxide into each of the cuts. I groaned and pounded the wall, trying not to shout as healing seared through my calf.

"Not in the hallway, dude," the desk guy called from around the corner, "or in the elevator. That thing is on its last leg."

Elizabeth rolled her eyes and pressed the button, making the doors open with a shudder. Wrapping her arm around me again, she half-dragged me into the elevator.

The subtle flickering of the lights sent bile flying into my throat as the elevator shook its way up, and the pain petered out.

"Do I look okay?" I asked as soon as I could open my mouth without fear of vomit.

Elizabeth took my chin in her hand and tipped my head around in the light.

"You look like you scratched your face too hard." She smiled and kissed my cheek, right where the cuts had been. "I think you just learned a new trick."

"I guess I did." I leaned in and kissed her. The world spun around me, or maybe the elevator was just super shaky, but time stopped, and I pulled Elizabeth in tighter. Her scent filled my lungs, and my heart galloped out of my chest.

The elevator *ding* yanked us out of eternity.

Elizabeth laced her fingers through mine, and we walked out of the elevator. With Elizabeth next to me, the dingy hall didn't seem so depressing. I couldn't smell old people and cheap cleaner, just fresh spring flowers.

"*Cliaxo*," I said, not wanting to let go of Elizabeth's hand to fish the keys out of my pocket. The keyhole turned, and the door swung open just in time for me to see my mom flop down onto the couch in an overly casual pose.

"Oh, Elizabeth!" Mom said brightly. "I didn't know the boys were meeting you."

"I caught up with them." Elizabeth smiled, bending to try and coax Mrs. Mops over to her.

"Did you have a nice walk with Devon?" Mom asked as Mrs. Mops growled at Elizabeth. The cat hadn't really trusted anyone but Mom since we abandoned her in the wreckage of our old apartment while we were running for our lives.

"I think he just needed some time to walk." Elizabeth pulled her hand out of Mrs. Mops' reach the second before she would have needed me to heal her with my new skills.

"I'm glad you all could spend some nice time together, doing normal things."

There was an awkward pause where my mom's disapproval of all things magical hung heavily in the air.

"Do your parents know you're out?" Mom looked at the clock in the corner. It was a big grandfather clock, which looked like it should be a family heirloom but in reality had been bought at a secondhand store when Mom was frantically scrambling to make this den of linoleum look homey.

"Sure," Elizabeth said a little too brightly. "I have another half hour till curfew."

It was a lie and I knew it, but I smiled along. The laundry list of things my mother didn't know grew by the second.

"Do you want Bryant to walk you home?" Mom offered. "I hate for you to be out alone at night."

"I'll take a cab."

I pulled out my wallet and grabbed a twenty. "Here." I passed the crisp bill to Elizabeth before Mom could come up with an argument against Elizabeth leaving alone.

"Thanks." Elizabeth rolled her eyes, playing the exasperated girlfriend of the rich kid perfectly.

"See you tomorrow, then." Mom headed to her bedroom, allowing Elizabeth and me a moment to say goodbye alone.

Elizabeth tried to pass the twenty back to me.

"Dad money." I shook my head. "Just keep it. And be careful."

"Always." Elizabeth brushed her lips gently against mine. "See you tomorrow."

My heart tightened in my chest as she shut the door. I leaned against the doorjamb, listening to her footsteps fading away.

I knew where she was going. To ride the subway. To sit on a dark corner. To watch the shadows and learn their secrets. She promised she was safe. So did Eric. They both said she was protected in a tone that meant I wasn't supposed to ask questions. But knowing the girl you're in love with is going to walk around Manhattan alone at night makes your heart panic, no matter who tells you she's safe.

When I couldn't hear her anymore, I went to the bathroom. The scratches on my face were barely visible. Little faint lines of pink cutting through the usual pastiness.

Elizabeth's parents thought she was interning backstage at a Broadway show. Another lie to another mom. Elizabeth wasn't practicing being a seer. Oh, no. She was living her theatrical dream. A horrible, unbelievable lie Devon and Eric had concocted.

Devon's parents thought I was going through a mid-teen crisis and Devon had become my personal handler. His parents hadn't bothered to ask if my having a nervous breakdown was going to be a bad influence on their son. They just let him stay out till all hours without question. Devon always seemed a little disappointed he hadn't been grounded for disappearing for hours at a time. He should have been the wizard. His parents wouldn't have minded him training with Eric. If they had even noticed.

Mom thought I was only meeting with Eric enough to fulfill my magical legal obligation of animal spell clean up and to learn enough magic to not accidentally blow myself up. She was super happy to let me wander around Manhattan with my girlfriend or best friend. Curfew didn't matter as long as there was no spell work involved.

And Dad...he thought his penthouse had been destroyed in a freak accident. He didn't know about the whole wizard thing at all.

It was so many lies to keep straight, thinking of it made my head pound and my half-frozen hands sweat.

All three of us had made the choice to be in the magical world. To learn and fight, to face danger and adventure. But the lying?

I don't think any of us had bargained for that.

4

"This isn't a proscenium stage," Mom's voice rang out over the actors who were being overly rambunctious for a 7:00 a.m. rehearsal. "You don't have the audience only on one side. The audience is surrounding you. You have to play to all sides."

"Excuse me, Ms. Miller," a tiny freshman piped in. "I thought you said we were supposed to cheat out so the audience could see us."

"You *were* supposed to cheat out when we had a stage." Mom's voice was a frightening mix of fatigue and frustration. "Our stage burned down, as I am sure you remember." All the theatre students nodded as one. "Since we don't have a stage, we are going to be performing in here." Mom swept her arms around, indicating the gym. She did it in an exciting and enthusiastic way that didn't show how depressing it really was to have moved from a giant theatre to a parquet-floored gym with acoustics only capable of making shoes squeal louder.

"Since we're going to be performing in here, we need to face all sides, we need to wear quiet shoes, and we need to project!" Mom had a manic look in her eyes, so I tuned out while she went on with the cleaning rehearsal for *A Christmas Carol*.

We should have been doing the show on the stage, but I accidentally burned down the whole theatre as my first act of magic. We should have been rehearsing after school when any of the poor actors had a shot at remembering their lines. I should have been sucking at helping my mom build a set, but there was no set to be built. Everything had turned into a pile of penniless theatrical poo after the fire, so I was painting signs for this afternoon's bake sale.

Wizard by night, cookie hawker by day. The oh-so-varied life of Bryant Jameson Adams.

They had gotten to the part where Elizabeth and Devon were both onstage. Devon was playing the young Ebenezer Scrooge and Elizabeth his love interest. For a minute, my stomach squirmed jealously as he knelt and proposed to Elizabeth, and I looked away as they kissed. It was weird—way, way weird—to have your best friend kiss your girlfriend. But better Devon than anyone else. Every other straight guy in school would kill to have Elizabeth Wick be their girlfriend. Devon was the only one I trusted to resist the lure of her sparkly eyes enough to not chase the girl of my dreams.

"Dammit," I cursed quietly as I looked at the sign I had been painting. The crooked letters now read *Cookis for sale.* I buried my face in my hands, half-tempted to search the phone for a way to erase paint, but it wasn't worth it. I chucked the sign and moved on to a new sheet of poster board.

I didn't get a chance to actually talk to Elizabeth or Devon until lunch. Devon and I had all our classes together, but they weren't really ideal places for conversation.

"You okay?" I asked Elizabeth as soon as she sat down at our table, her tray laden with something that looked like it could be spaghetti and meatballs if you weren't really sure what spaghetti and meatballs were supposed to be.

"I'm golden." Elizabeth smiled tiredly and snuck a bottle of coffee out of her bag, adding in a whisper. "The life juice of seers."

"Did you actually *see* anything?" Devon murmured after looking casually around. He did it well, like he was searching for a cute girl to hit on instead of prying ears.

"A few creepy crawlies." Elizabeth shrugged. "Nothing of any real interest."

"And you were safe?" I pulled my lunch out of its bag. I had been in the back of the faculty meeting where they discussed the health department almost shutting down the cafeteria a month before, and I hadn't been able to eat the food since.

"I was safe." Elizabeth nodded. "I was the safest girl in Manhattan."

"Except for the people who weren't out looking for things that go bump in the night and were tucked safely in their warm beds." Devon waved a French fry. "They were probably safer."

"Please don't mention beds." Elizabeth lifted her coffee, but before it could reach her mouth, a beefy hand caught it.

"What is this?" The evil lunch lady towered behind Elizabeth, her wide face twisted in a quasi-comical frown.

"My drink," Elizabeth growled, not releasing her grip on the glass bottle.

"The school board doesn't want coffee or soda in this school." The lunch lady's grating, low voice made the nerves in my neck twitch.

It was true though. A bunch of parents had banded together to get soda, coffee, and all things joyful banned from the school. They had ranted about negative health effects and concentration in class. Kids could pound a latte on the sidewalk, but pass through the school doors, and it was no coffee allowed.

"I'm so sorry," Elizabeth said, speaking in a cheerful tone through clenched teeth. "I totally forgot. But I mixed my medicine with it, so now I really need to drink it."

With a tug of her beefy hand the lunch lady yanked the coffee from Elizabeth's grasp, splashing the front of her shirt with brown. "I'm sure the nurse has your medicine in stock." The lunch lady grinned like a Cheshire cat, showing her yellowed teeth.

"You just splashed her." I leapt chivalrously to my girlfriend's defense. "You could at least say sorry."

The lunch lady's eyes flashed to me. She looked from my unruly hair to my clenched hands, and her smile grew. "How nice to find a hero in the lunchroom." With a laugh like she was hocking up phlegm, she turned and waddled away, holding her prize above her head for all to see.

"That woman truly is evil." Elizabeth's voice shook as she tried to sponge the coffee from her shirt with a flimsy paper napkin.

"If only you could tell her you needed the caffeine to stay awake after prowling the city by night to try and find the next big bad who wants to bring destruction and death down on all of us." Devon glared after the lunch lady.

"Move your hands," I whispered.

Elizabeth moved her hands and leaned toward me.

"*Nudla.*" I spoke the word below a whisper. With a *hiss*, the stain vanished.

"My boyfriend, the magical dry cleaner." Elizabeth kissed me on the cheek.

"Not in my cafeteria!" the lunch lady hollered.

Elizabeth sat back, grinding her teeth loud enough for me to hear.

"Are we all set for the bake sale?" Devon asked. I think he was more trying to distract Elizabeth from throwing her tray at the coffee thief than actually concerned about the cookies.

"We have everything in order." Elizabeth's jaw gradually loosened as she spoke so she wasn't talking through her teeth.

"There are posters lining the halls. The cash box and merchandise are ready in Ms. Miller's office. And all of us will be released early from our last classes to sell at the final bell."

"Then move to the sidewalk to freeze while we sell the extras." Devon nodded. "I love live theatre."

My phone buzzed in my pocket. Not the magic one, the normal one.

I pulled it out under the table, careful not to let the lunch lady see in case she decided it was cafeteria contraband.

A text message showed on the screen.

You should be on lunch. Come outside now. Tell no one.

You would think the message had come from Eric or a mob boss. But there was a little tag underneath.

~Dad

My mind went blank for a second, then raced to think of what I possibly could have done to make my dad come see me at school. Or, more likely, send someone to come see me at school. Ever since Eric and I had fought an epic battle that destroyed my dad's penthouse that he still didn't know I was mostly responsible for, I had been on my best behavior.

Unless my dad had finally found out it was me who destroyed his home.

My stomach dropped past my butt and shattered. I stood up slowly, my legs shaking.

"Are you okay?" Devon asked. "You just got super pale, Bry."

"Oh God, is it venom?" Elizabeth turned white. "Does Nutty have venom?"

"What was on your phone?" Devon asked.

"A-a," I stammered dumbly. "A reminder I had a project. I set it for the wrong time. I forgot my paper. I'm gonna see if Mom can print it." I turned and ran out of the cafeteria before either of them could argue with my ridiculously lame and unbelievable excuse.

The weight of another set of lies twisted the shards of my shattered stomach.

I slowed my speed as I walked down the hall toward the front door of the school. I wasn't technically forbidden to go outside during lunch, but if I acted like something was wrong, I could get stopped.

It might seem weird that I was so freaked out about my dad asking me to meet him outside, and it wasn't just the cryptic message. Seeing my dad wasn't like a weekly or even monthly ritual. He was always away doing important business things. Most of my time with him over the last few years consisted of grabbing a coffee on one of his infrequent visits to the city. But since his penthouse got wrecked, he'd been in town more often than usual. Once to file the insurance claim, then to meet with a realtor, then to sign the papers on his new fancy brownstone. Unless he was here to purchase a priceless antique rug to go with the vibe of his new place, there was no reasonable explanation for him coming back so soon.

I made it out the front door without any more than a suspicious glare from the ancient biology teacher. For a second, I expected my dad to be standing outside, but he wasn't. And there wasn't a fancy black car waiting obtrusively in front of the school either. As I looked around, my phone buzzed in my hand.

Turn left.

I squinted down the street. At the far end of the block was a big black car.

"Great," I muttered, keeping my head down against the wind as it tore through my sweater.

I walked as fast as I could without looking like I was trying to escape from high school. As soon as I reached the car, the back door swung open, and a familiar voice said, "You should've stopped to get your coat, Bryant. You're going to freeze to death out here."

He didn't want me dead. That was a good sign.

"You said now." I slid into the backseat of the car and closed the door, keeping in the precious warmth.

Dad pulled me into an awkward side hug, ruffling my hair like I was still five. It only lasted for a moment, and then he leaned back in his seat looking cool and calm as ever. My dad was the opposite of me. Blue eyes, black curly hair just long enough to make him look like a Hollywood star, and a chiseled jaw to complete the Greek god look.

"How are you, Bryant?" Dad asked. "School going all right?"

"Yeah, fine." It wasn't his real question, and I knew it.

"Excellent." Dad smiled. "And how is your mother's new apartment?"

We were getting closer to it now.

"Not as homey as the old one, but it works." I shrugged, trying not to betray how much I hated the linoleum. "The neighborhood is good, and we have an elevator."

That might get all of us killed.

"It's amazing how much real estate is available in this area if you know where to look." Dad's tone was all contemplative, like he was just coming to a remarkable conclusion. "I bet there are some excellent places to be found—"

"If mom would only use your realtor?" I finished for him. "She's never going to go for it, Dad."

"Buying is a wise investment."

"She doesn't have money for a down payment." I felt like a traitor saying it out loud. That's the problem with having one super rich parent and one normal one—it's hard for them to understand each other. Mom was doing fine, but not fine enough to buy a two bedroom in Manhattan.

"She wouldn't need one," Dad said. "Not if she had someone willing to co-sign on the loan."

"No." I shook my head so hard the leather interior of the car went blurry. "No, no, no, no, no. Never in a billion years would Mom let you co-sign a loan for her. No."

"I want you to at least mention it." Dad passed me a shiny black folder. "There are ten properties in this area that would work well for you two. And the mortgage wouldn't be more than your mother is paying in rent with the right kind of loan."

"We're fine."

"This is as much for her as it is for you. You'll be off to college soon, but your mother will still be in the city. She'll probably retire a teacher in the Manhattan school system. Her life will be easier if she owns an apartment. At least try and convince her. It's for her own good."

"But..." I wanted to say no again and toss the folder on the floor of the car, but the *but* was he was right. If she could own a place of her own....

"And how is the theatre reconstruction going?" Dad pressed on, apparently unaware of the deep-seeded issues I was trying to sort through.

"Good, fine. The school had a ton of insurance." I tried not to let my mind wander to how much I had cost the insurance industry with my badly used magic. "It's going to take some time for all of it to come in and for reconstruction to start. We're doing some fundraisers to rent show stuff and a space for the performances until they can build a new theatre."

"I've heard as much."

"From who?"

Dad didn't answer. Instead, he reached down and pulled out a lunch bag. One of the kind that's tapered at the top like a folded over paper bag but is really made of fabric and insulation.

"Finding a space in Manhattan isn't easy or cheap." Dad set the lunch bag on top of the folder on my lap.

Hands shaking, I opened the bag. A mound of money sat inside. "How much?"

"A hundred thousand," Dad said like it was nothing. Like he really was just giving me lunch money.

"No, Dad, no." I tried to push the bag back. "She won't take it."

"She will if she doesn't know it's from me." Dad closed the top of the bag and shoved it back toward me. "You're working the bake sale. Slip it in with the rest of the money at the end of the day."

"'Cause that won't be suspicious."

"It doesn't matter if it's suspicious. If she can't prove it's from me, she'll have to take it." Dad grinned, and for a second I could almost picture him as the young idealist my mom had fallen in love with in Bryant Park.

"Why?" I begged. "Why do you, do *I*, have to do this? She'll be fine on her own. We'll figure it out somehow. We always have."

"Your mother and I may not always agree, and we definitely don't get along, but she is the mother of my son, and I want her to have a decent place to grow old in." He pressed the folder to my chest. "And she is an amazing teacher who has spent too much time building this program to let it crumble."

"Dad."

"I have more money than I could possibly use." He held a hand up so I wouldn't interrupt. "Don't argue with me because I want to do something good with it. Why should I be blamed if the good has to do with my family?"

"She won't go for the apartment." I felt my fight deflating like a shriveled-up balloon of dying hope.

"I'm only asking you to try."

"She'll know the money came from you."

"She won't be able to prove it."

"This is such a bad idea." I buried my face in my cold hands.

"It's a brilliant idea, Bryant. You'll see." He reached across me and opened to car door. "Now get back in there and try to learn something."

"Thanks, Dad." I stepped back into the cold. "I'll try."

"Good. I love you, Son." With a wave, my dad shut the door and the car pulled away, not pausing for me to call *I love you* back.

5

I stood on the sidewalk for a second, holding a folder of real estate printouts in one hand and a hundred thousand dollars in the other. It wasn't until I started shivering that I realized I really should go back inside.

Back inside and do what? Put the money in my locker and leave it until the end of the day?

"Dammit, Dad."

I turned to go back inside, but a wall of black blocked me.

"Do you really think it wise to be walking around outside without a coat?" Eric asked, one black eyebrow arched high on his alabaster forehead. "Have you decided to use a little trick from the phone to keep warm? It might draw unnecessary attention, but I applaud your embracing magic."

"I came out here to talk to my dad."

"The mystery father appeared?" Eric looked up and down the street as though hoping to catch a glimpse of him.

"Just because you've never met him doesn't mean he's a mystery." I started my trudge back to school.

"No, your lack of understanding of your patriarch makes

him a mystery. And where do you think you're going?" Eric stepped in front of me.

"Back to school." I pointed over Eric's shoulder. "Back to slave away in my brick prison."

"I hate to ruin your plans for education, but I'm afraid there is other urgent business that needs tending to."

"What business?"

Eric took his phone from his pocket and pulled up a picture —a three-headed deer running across the GW Bridge.

"Oh sh—" I won't write out all the curses that flew from my mouth.

"This picture appeared on the Internet after one of your little casualties made a bid for freedom and caused quite a stir."

"Did it get hit?"

"Did it get hit? There are more important things to attend to than your bleeding heart, and no, we have no idea where the animal is." Eric's normally creepily blue eyes had gone dark. I had recently begun to recognize this as a sign he was going to get really serious about something I didn't understand. "We can only hope fate guided the beast as far from Manhattan as the thing can run. If the creature is going to stay in the wild, the farther from us it is, the better. They can call it a genetic anomaly or blame a plague or chemicals for the creature's existence."

"B-but that's g-good right?" I asked through chattering teeth. "I-I mean th-that leaves only one m-more left to find."

"Leaves one more left to find, but has, in all likelihood, alerted the Ladies to your misconduct."

For the second time that hour my stomach dropped clear out of my body. "What does that mean?"

"It means we can no longer allow you to learn while you search for the animals." Eric took my shoulders and steered me down the street. "It means the Ladies now have a legitimate reason to come after you. It means the terrible feeling that has been creeping into the corners of my life that something is waiting just out of sight to come after us is probably correct."

"Something else is coming after us? Like not Ladies or deer?" I pictured giant shadow monsters creeping out of the sewer and grabbing my ankles, dragging me farther underground than Beville, to swampy places of shadows and death. I dug in my heels, refusing to let Eric push me any farther.

"We have had two months of unnatural peace. Are you really surprised that placidity has come to an end?"

"Well, I was kind of hoping non-deadly fun had become our new thing." We stopped in front of the school steps. The few lunchtime stragglers braving the cold stared at me.

"Fate laughs at hope," Eric said. "We have things to attend to, Bryant. Now let's go."

I glanced from the folder in one hand to the lunch bag in the other. "Can I run in and get my coat? Just really quickly? I'm freezing." It wasn't a lie. I was frozen to the bone. I also didn't want to carry enough money to buy a small house in Upstate around the city with me while we searched Central Park for whatever animal I had accidentally altered.

"You want a coat? Fine." Eric muttered something under his breath I couldn't hear then reached into his pocket.

It was the most magician-like thing I had seen him do. It was like that trick where a dude in a top hat pulls a hundred scarves out of your mouth or ear. Only Eric was dragging something made of black wool out of his pocket. In a few seconds, he shook the fabric, showing a replica of his own black trench coat.

"Here." Eric strode down the street, leaving me gaping at the newly-fashioned coat.

I swore some more under my breath, yanked on the coat, and chased after him. It was a long coat that was perfectly tailored...for Eric. On me, the sleeves hung over my hands, and the shoulders sagged past my armpits. But it had a pocket deep enough for the black folder to lay rolled up in. As for the money bag, I did the safest thing I could think of and shoved it down the back of my pants. I'd had too much experience with pickpockets to leave something like that in an open pocket.

"Are you warm enough to preserve our magical lives now?" Eric asked when I caught up to him.

"It's very nice. Thank you." I tried to keep the sarcasm out of my tone.

"Just think of how well you could look if you visited a proper tailor. Then you could truly fit in on the streets of Beville."

"My life's dreams fulfilled," I said.

"I think the best place to start would be the castle." Eric dodged between cars in a way that would have given my mother a heart attack. I followed, trusting Eric to not let me die. "It may seem cliché, but that is a very likely place. Or perhaps by the water."

"What if the thing is already dead and mounted on someone's wall as a creepy trophy?" I asked as we weaved around a bunch of old ladies fighting over which bodega they should go to.

"While we can hope for that, we can't count on it," Eric said. "Fortunately, I have a friend meeting us who should be able to make quick work of finding the thing."

"A friend?" I wasn't sure if I should be excited or terrified.

"I hate to make him come out in the light, and favors will be owed, but such is the work to be done."

"You're going to owe someone a favor?" I had forgotten to walk for a few seconds, so I had to run to catch up. "Isn't owing a favor, like, a much bigger deal for magical types than for non-demented humans?"

"A debt left unpaid can chase a wizard into death itself."

"And you owe someone because of me?" My voice squeaked as I spoke. "You shouldn't have done...whatever it is you did."

We had reached the edge of the park, and Eric headed north.

"I am your mentor, and you are my apprentice. If the Ladies come after you for breaches of the magical code, then they will come after me as well. Your conduct reflects on me." Eric stopped and rounded on me so quickly I rammed right into him. "I am doing this for both of us, Bryant, and the source isn't such a terrible one to owe."

"Still, thanks."

Eric slapped me a little too hard on the shoulder and turned to study the street.

There wasn't all that much to see. The middle west side of Central Park isn't exactly a tourist hot spot on a freezing winter day. There were a few hardy folks trudging along, taking pictures of the leafless trees and snow-spotted grass. Natives hurried past, heads tucked down against the cold. And one sad bundle of filthy, mismatched clothes huddled against the wall.

"Here we are." Eric walked right up to the bundle of rags.

I hoped the mass of fabric wouldn't look up. I hoped there wasn't a person hiding under there. But the rags stirred, and a face appeared. A sad little fist clenched around my heart. It was a kid. He couldn't have been more than ten. His eyes looked vacant, like two glassy nothings above his sunken cheeks.

"I'm glad you were able to meet us." Eric gave a little bow as the boy stood.

The boy nodded and turned his eyes toward me. Recognition trickled through my brain.

"I've seen you before. At Lola's...you're one of Lola's guards."

The boy nodded, and a shiver swept up my spine. He looked like a child, a very hungry, dirty child. But I knew that wasn't true. Elizabeth could see Lola's guards as they truly were—rotting corpses of something not quite human.

The boy walked toward me. I clenched my fists to keep my hands from shaking. The boy leaned in toward me, looking for all the world like an animal sniffing, then he looked up to Eric.

"You're quite right." Eric smiled, though the expression didn't reach his eyes. "He does spend a considerable amount of time with Miss Wick."

"Elizabeth?"

Eric shot me a look that very clearly said *Don't ask questions right now*, so I bit my lips together and stayed silent.

"As we've finished introductions, perhaps we should get down to business." Eric moved toward the entrance to the park where a wide swath of asphalt created a walking path. "We're looking for a creature, hopefully small, though it is not necessarily so. It has been transformed in some way by this boy—"

I ruffled a little inside at being called *boy*.

"That is really the best information I have for you."

We were under the trees now. The winter sun fought its way through the bare branches, trying to liven up the mostly dead park.

"I have been assured you can make quick work in finding such a thing?" Eric paused to look at the kid as though waiting for some silent communication.

The boy/undead shadow monster tipped his head to the side for a second before rounding on me. He didn't even bother creeping closer this time. He walked right over and started sniffing me. He grabbed both my hands, so quickly I wasn't sure how to react, and took a good whiff of my palms. His hands were freezing, colder than the air or ice. Colder than any living thing should ever be. But then, the kid wasn't really living.

The boy turned and walked down the sidewalk before cutting north through the grass.

"Keep up, Bryant," Eric called over his shoulder as I ran to follow.

The lunch bag of money slipped down my pants, and I stumbled as I reached to hike it back up. The last thing I needed was a small fortune falling out the leg of my pants.

The kid sprinted in front of us. It was just like chasing a dog. He would sprint for stretches then stop and stand very still for a few seconds before taking off again. It didn't seem to matter what parts of the park we weren't supposed to enter either. The boy ducked under chains and leapt over fences in an unnatural way, leaving Eric and me scrambling behind him. Okay, Eric wasn't scrambling. He was running behind the undead kid like it was nothing. I was scrambling and trying not to fall on the ice while balancing money in the back of my boxer briefs.

"Why?" I panted when the sniffer dog stopped to stare at a bush after running us east for a few minutes. "Why are we just doing this now? Why didn't we kill the bad guy, win the battle, ask the favor, and catch the weird oopsie animals two months ago?"

"It was your place to clean it up on your own." Stupid Eric wasn't panting. "To rebalance the scales of magic as it were. You make the mess, you clean it up. Simple as that."

"Is this going to turn into some big fate thing now where I'm going to get my ass handed to me because you helped me?" Not gonna lie, it came out really whiny.

"Probably."

The boy snaked his way into the bush, squeezing between barren branches.

"But it's better to need to find a way to right the scales of magic than to give the Ladies a new reason to come after us."

Sniffer McDeadDog leapt back out of the bush and started running again.

"Can't I do, like, magical community service or something?" I panted between gasping breaths. "Help old ladies cross the dangerous streets of Beville?"

"Do you think *you* could survive the dangerous streets of Beville?" Eric turned to look at me, running backward with one black eyebrow perfectly arched.

"Isn't there anything?"

"We'll know when it comes." He started running forward again just as Sniffer stopped in his tracks, pointing high up in a tree.

6

A *bird.*

That was my first thought. I had made furry, many-headed bird. Then I noticed it didn't have wings. Then it hissed and moved farther forward on the branches.

Fear curdled my intestines as my mind floundered, failing to find a way to put the horror into reasonable terms.

"Rat king!" I screamed. "It's a rat king!"

The thing startled at the noise and swiveled its nine heads toward me.

That's right. Nine freakin' heads!

I stumbled backward, landing hard on my butt. I scooted back across the frozen ground as the thing undulated down the tree. It was worse than I had ever imagined, even after hearing the urban legends that give nightmares to every New York kid with a healthy self-preservation instinct. Nine rats joined together by a tangle of tails crept down the tree toward us. But the tails weren't joined by gunk or glue. They had melded together into one, veiny disk so it looked like a fleshy Frisbee had sprouted rats.

The nine weren't moving independently either. They

were moving as one, inching down the tree, staring at me like they were being controlled by one brain. The rats were all the same size. Too big to be normal, too small to make moving as a unit impossible. But the most terrifying thing of all was the one pure white rat who seemed to be the host of the others' thoughts. Leading the path down the tree, swiveling his head toward the undead boy a split second before the others.

The boy rounded his shoulders, looking like he would have growled if he ever made noise.

The rat king looked to Eric who said in an overly calm voice. "The coloring does seem symbolic, doesn't it?"

"What?" I screeched. Big mistake—it made the thing look back at me.

"Well, Bryant." Eric stepped aside, leaving a wide path between the nine-headed monster and me. "We've helped you find the beast. Now catch him."

"Nope!" The scream tore from my throat as I leapt to my feet. "Nope. Not going near it."

The evil, disgusting monster chittered as it reached solid ground.

"Bryant, just trap the thing," Eric said tiredly.

But I couldn't remember a spell. I couldn't think of any words. So again I shouted, "Nope!"

I ran backward a few steps. I wanted to run all the way to Brooklyn, but I couldn't bring myself to look away from the monster's eighteen beady, black eyes.

"Bryant, you're being rather ridiculous."

Something heavy fell down the leg of my pants, slowing my progress as I stumbled over it. "No, no, no!"

The thing was only five feet from me.

"What the hell is that?" A voice spoke from somewhere behind me, and other voices answered.

"Wonderful." Eric sighed. "Bryant, we really need to be done here."

Done. I wanted to be done. I wanted the rat to be dead.

In a fit of theatre-bred frenzy, I remembered the Nutcracker and that little girl killing a giant mouse with her shoe. I reached down to pull off my sneaker, but there was something else on the ground. A nice, heavy, sturdy-looking bag.

I picked up the bag and threw it at the rat king. It hit him straight in the Frisbee of conjoined tails, making the thing scream as hundred dollar bills flew into the air.

"Money!" a voice screamed behind me. There were other words, too.

"Is it real?"

"Get it!"

"Watch out for the rat!"

"Stop!" I shouted at the top of my lungs. I didn't know what I was telling to stop, the rat king that was only a few feet from me, or the people trying to get to my dad's illicit bake sale money.

The monster hissed, baring its teeth.

"Oh dear." Eric tipped his head down, looking like I was the most disappointing thing in the history of the world as random people charged toward me, braving the rat for a chance at money. "*Dothranta.*"

Everything went black. If the people charging toward my dad's money hadn't started screaming, I might've.

There was a hissing sound, then screeching as something thumped to the ground. It might seem cowardly, but I didn't step toward the shrill *squeal*. I backed away, careful not to fall. With a *crack* and a *thump*, the screeching stopped, but the people were still screaming.

Someone banged into me, knocking me to the ground.

"Eric!" I shouted, hoping he would have a way to see in his darkness. "Eric!"

He didn't answer, but a hand grabbed the back of my jacket, hauling me to my feet.

"Eric?"

I could almost feel my legs again, but the hand dragged me back so quickly I couldn't keep my feet under me. As I fumbled toward the ground, the sun burst back into being. "What the hell?" I twisted around and fell to the ground. "Eric..." But it wasn't Eric who had hauled me out of the dark. It was the boy, gripping my coat in one hand and the bloody, dead rat king in the other. I screamed and rolled away, catching a glimpse of Eric walking toward me, holding my lunch bag in his hand.

But the people behind him weren't chasing the bag of money. They were still stumbling around in a panic like they couldn't see anything.

"You saved the money?" I panted.

"I wasn't about to let the masses take it." Eric tossed the bag, and it landed at my feet. "With any luck, it's all in there."

With a squishing *thunk*, the undead boy threw the very dead rat king at my feet.

"Why!" I leapt to my feet, clutching the lunch bag and trying not to vomit. Each of the rat's nine necks had been snapped. At least, their spines didn't look right anymore, so I assumed that was what had happened.

"Thank you for disposing of the creature." Eric bowed to the boy. "You went above and beyond our agreement. I won't forget it."

The boy stared at Eric.

"We are done," Eric said.

The boy turned and shambled down the park, any indication he could run completely gone.

"We should leave before the spell breaks," Eric said.

I glanced at the people groping around in the dark.

"What about that?" I pointed to the rat king corpse with a sinking feeling Eric would want me to pick it up.

"Can't you at least get rid of that much yourself?" Eric pressed a knuckle to the bridge of his nose.

I pulled the black phone out of my pocket and held my thumb to the scanner. The screen flashed on. I tapped on the icon that looked like fire. A level bar balanced beneath blackened logs blinked into being. Pointing the phone like I was going to take a picture of the pile of mangled rat, I pulled the bar all the way to the right.

With a smell that would make a sewer cleaner gag, a pillar of fire five feet high sprang to life. I covered my mouth and nose with the rich man's lunch bag and counted to ten before sliding the bar back to the left.

The fire poofed out, leaving nothing but a scorched circle of earth to mark the death of the rat king.

"Well done, Bryant." Eric didn't look proud. "Now let's go." He took off at a brisk trot, heading south the same way the boy had gone.

I ran after him, hoping the wind would blow the stink of burned rat off me.

It was over. We had dealt with the three animals. Nutty McDragon had found a home and a new career as a mangler extraordinaire, the deer was hopefully living it up peacefully in Upstate, and the rat from hell was dead.

I tripped over my feet as a guilty weight thumped into my stomach. I would be mad if someone hurt Nutty even though he had tried to take a chunk out of my face, but I was thrilled the rat was dead. I packed that moral quandary away for another time and bolted after Eric.

Once we were well out of sight of the rat king's funeral pyre, Eric changed his pace to a stroll. I skidded to a stop behind him.

"How long will those people think they're in the dark?" I puffed.

"They are in the dark," Eric said. "It's just a one-way darkness. It should be gone in the next few minutes."

"What are they going to say happened? Do you think they'll call the police?"

I didn't want to think of how giddy the Ladies would be if they found out I had messed up badly enough that a bunch of normal people got caught in a one-way darkness spell.

"They'll call for an ambulance before they call the police." Eric didn't seem too worried, so I let my fear go a bit. "There is no crime any of them will be able to think of that could take away the light. They'll come up with some fancy medical name for it and leave us well alone."

"Then it's done." I heaved a sigh of relief, letting the cold air of the park wash away my anxiety. "All I have to do is deliver this to the bake sale and I'll be good." I shoved the lunch bag back down the back of my pants.

"Indeed." Eric's voice sounded dark when he said it, like he didn't think we were done at all.

"Don't *indeed*," I begged. "Please, don't *indeed*. Haven't we done enough for one day?"

"We have by all measure. Now it's just a matter of if the day is done with us."

"What does that mean?" The question came out as a whimper.

"Have you ever had the feeling someone was watching you?" Eric turned onto a side path away from the rest of the people around us. "That there are eyes staring at the back of your neck?"

"Of course, everyone feels that sometimes."

"But have you ever felt the truth of it?" Eric turned down

another path. "Known for certain there is someone waiting for a moment of weakness to strike?"

I wanted to say no, he was being paranoid, but I knew the exact feeling he was talking about. "When I had the phone, before I knew you weren't evil, it felt like a giant eye was watching me."

"Thaden was watching, and you were wise enough to know." Eric turned again, cutting back through the grass toward the edge of the park. "I've had the feeling of something creeping closer for days—"

"But we fixed it," I cut across him. "We got rid of the last bit of my mistake. It's all okay. The Ladies can't come after us for that now."

"We arranged a battle that killed most of their number. The Ladies coming for us is inevitable. Getting rid of the animals was only a means of postponement. They can't admit we caused the battle without admitting we still have the phone and acknowledging the triumph of Charles and his people."

I shuddered at the thought of Charles, a man made shadow, who risked everything to fight the Ladies and Thaden in the battle of Beville.

"They will find a reason to come for us."

"Maybe years and years from now, right?" I asked as we cut back out of the park and onto the sidewalk. "You said maybe years!"

"Or they might send someone else after us." Eric looked back over his shoulder and toward the park. "I've not heard of it happening, but I wouldn't be surprised if, weakened as they are, they turn to outsourcing."

"Outsourcing?" I screamed the word. "You think they want to outsource our murders?"

"There are three options I can think of, Bryant." He cut into the lobby of a fancy apartment building. Before the woman at the front desk could pop up to ask how she could help us, Eric led me through the marble-floored hall and out the side door into a courtyard. "Option number one: I have lost my touch. I no longer have a keen sense for impending danger, which leaves us open to a multitude of enemies yet unknown." Eric burst through the doors of a restaurant and strode straight through it and into the kitchen, scaring the poop out of the dishwashers as we cut back out to the street.

"Option two: The Ladies have decided that, rather than wait for a justified offense we have committed they want to admit to, they will hire someone to rid themselves of us without worrying about messy legalities, which leaves us open to attack from any scum who can do a spell and is looking to earn a few extra dollars in this sad world."

We ran down the steps to a subway station and back out the other side.

"Option three: There is another source that wants us dead. A person or entity yet unknown has decided Manhattan would be better off without us. And this, Bryant, is the most troubling possibility of all." Eric turned on me so suddenly I nearly tipped over trying to stop before I rammed into him. "This means someone we are unaware of is willing to use time and resources we cannot estimate to destroy us. Manhattan has just become a very dangerous place."

7

W e spent the next half hour running in circles back to my school. I ran with my hand on the back of my pants, trying to make sure I didn't lose the money again. Eric wanted me to dash into school really quickly, grab Elizabeth and Devon, and run for the (relative) safety of Beville. But with the bake sale and, you know, school, there was no way to grab them without the faculty and my mom knowing we had all escaped.

"Try not to get into any life-threatening trouble," Eric ordered as he left me on the school steps.

I had missed all the time left before the bake sale, so all I had to do was walk nonchalantly through the halls with a ton of money in my underpants, hoping no one could smell the burnt rat carcass on my new magically-made coat.

Elizabeth was already at the table, laying out rows of cookies, brownies, and other sweet treats.

"Hi," I whispered as I reached her.

"Bryant." She threw her arms around my neck like she hadn't seen me in months. "Where the hell have you been? Your mom found out you were gone, and she's been flipping out." Elizabeth stepped back and slugged me in the arm. "She's been trying to call you. Devon and I have been trying to call you! Why the hell didn't you answer your phone?"

I reached into my pants pocket and pulled out my non-magic phone. Twelve missed calls from Mom, Devon, and Elizabeth.

"Damn. I didn't even feel it. I mean, there was sort of a lot going on."

"What's in your pants?" Elizabeth leaned to look behind me where I was still clutching the lunch bag.

"Don't freak out," I said.

Elizabeth tensed like I was about to pull the rat king out of my pants. Not that she knew I had almost been murdered by a rat king. I passed her the lunch bag and mouthed *open it.* Because mouthing is less suspicious, obviously.

"Jesus, Bryant." Her sparkly eyes got all wide. "Where the hell did you get this?"

"Dad. He wants me to dump it in with the bake sale money." I pulled Elizabeth around to the backside of the table as the bell rang and students appeared in the hall.

"What the hell is he thinking?" Elizabeth whisper-screamed.

"He really is trying to help." I ran a frozen hand over my face. "He wants to help the theatre program."

"And your mom isn't going to know exactly where this came from?"

"Bryant Jameson Adams." Mom's voice echoed down the hall.

Elizabeth shoved the lunch bag into my chest and I tossed it back to her.

"I'm not taking it!" Elizabeth yelped.

"Please!"

Mom was halfway down the hall, glaring at me with her laser eyes.

Please, I mouthed.

With a panicked glare, Elizabeth shoved the lunch bag under the table.

"Bryant, where on God's green earth did you disappear to?" Mom's voice was crazy calm and pleasant, but her eyes were furious.

"I-I." I had two choices: half truth or all lie.

"You were with him, weren't you?" Mom took my arm and dragged me out of the hallway and into an empty classroom. I caught one last glance of Elizabeth looking panicky before the door shut, locking me in with the mom monster.

"What makes you think leaving school to run around with him is in any way acceptable?"

The use of the word *him* was problematic. I could surmise she meant Eric, which was reasonable since I saw him a lot more than I saw my dad. But if someone said they had seen me get into a big black car she would know it was my dad. I needed more information.

"It was an emergency."

"What sort of emergency requires the attention of my sixteen-year-old son?" Mom's eyes glittered dangerously. "What task was so insurmountable that only you, and not responsible adults, could handle it?"

"It wasn't really an emergency per se." I back-peddled. "More like a time-sensitive thing that ended up taking longer than I thought it would."

"And what was this urgent matter that was more important than school?"

She had me again. I still didn't know which *him*. I took a risk and pulled the black folder out of my pocket. "Dad wanted me to give you this." The rolled up folder glinted in the light.

She pinched her lips together.

I had gotten it right.

She opened the folder and glared at the pages.

"The urgent situation was real estate?" Her voice was tight and strained. A bad sign, a very bad sign.

Time to Mom detonation: 10, 9, 8...

"He wanted me to show you the apartments his realtor found."

"And he thinks your lowly mother can afford any of these?"

6,5,4...

"He wants to help you buy it so you can have money to retire." I started backing toward the door. "He really does seem like he wants to help."

3,2...

I reached for the doorknob, hoping against hope I could slip out the door and run before she blew.

"Bryant Jameson Adams, why the hell is there blood on your shoes?"

Boom!

I froze with my hand on the doorknob and glanced down. Splashes of rat king blood dotted the orange and white of my shoes. I bent over and puked on the floor.

"Bryant!" Mom pulled me away from my own vomit. "What the hell is going on?"

"There was a rat king." My defenses were gone. "One of the animals I changed turned out to be a rat king and we had to chase it and I got blood on my shoes."

"And what about the folder?" Mom growled and waved the folder in the air.

"Dad gave it to me." I was going to pass out. All I could think of was the rat blood on my shoes. I needed to burn my shoes. That was clearly the only option. Amputating my feet might be necessary, too.

Mom went silent.

The smell of my puke made me gag again.

"Grounded." She pronounced it like a verdict. "You are

grounded. No going out. No magic. I can't keep you from seeing your father, but I will be making sure he doesn't pull you out of school again."

"Yes, Mom." I knew I should say something about how I couldn't walk away from magic since there might be people trying to kill me, but when your mom is bearing down on you, you can't really fight back.

"Go home now. Get your books, and go home. No stops, no talking to anyone, straight home."

"Yes, Mom." I turned and headed for the door.

"Wait."

I turned back around.

Mom had her hand held out. "Phone."

I pulled my phone out of my pocket and handed it to her.

"The other one, too."

My heart skipped a beat. I needed that phone. I needed to protect myself and my friends.

"I need it." I shook my head. "I need to keep it with me."

"Why? What is going on that you need to keep the phone?"

Another battle raged in my exhausted brain. I needed the phone to fight whatever was following us. If I told my mom something was coming, she would either want us to flee the country or come up with some other crazy plan to protect me. Last time she had tried to save me from a magical problem, she almost ended up dead.

"There's nothing going on," I lied, and bile crept back up into my throat. "The animals are all gone so there's nothing going on."

"Then give it to me." Mom held her hand out again.

I pulled out the magical phone. It seemed heavier in my hand than it ever had before.

Mom stared at me, waiting for me to pass it over. My heart raced. I hadn't been without the phone in two months. I kept it with me always. A defense against the shadows, and Ladies, and death in general.

"Bryant."

Everything blurred as I placed the one-of-a-kind magical library contained in a portable device in my mom's hand.

"Now go."

Mom didn't know my head was spinning out of control. She just stood there, mom-glaring at me like she had taken away a video game controller.

"We'll discuss the length of your grounding when I get home."

I nodded. My mouth was too dry to say words. I opened the door to the hall, which had flooded with students. A mob surrounded the bake sale table. Elizabeth and Devon were barely visible behind the horde. I wanted to dive through the crowd and make sure Elizabeth hadn't been attacked for the giant bag of money. But I could feel Mom's eyes on the back of my neck. I would just have to trust Elizabeth and Devon to guard the money and my mom to keep the phone safe. She wouldn't get rid of it. She couldn't.

My hands felt fuzzy as I pulled my real coat and bag from my locker. Like maybe losing the phone had drained me of magic, and losing my magic had made my body numb.

But that wasn't how it worked. I was still magical. I was still Bryant Adams, boy wizard. I was just...helpless.

The streets were packed on the walk home. Hundreds of strangers surrounded me, and my one defense was gone. Every old lady felt like a terrible threat. Every businessman ditching work early had some evil, magical thing hidden in his briefcase. The kids running past me on their way home were goblins in disguise. I didn't even know if goblins existed, but I was absolutely sure those kids were evil.

I wanted to bolt for Columbus Circle and head straight for

Beville. Tell Eric my mom had confiscated the dangerous magical device and make him fix it. But she would know I had gone to him. Then she would know something was wrong, and she would get hurt.

I took off at a run. Not heading for Beville, but back to the linoleum-floored apartment. Back to my bedroom, which I still felt like I was visiting. I dodged between tourists and locals, not letting the squeals of alarm or curses of frustration slow me down. I tore through the lobby and pounded the janky elevator button until the damn thing rattled to the first floor.

The doors dinged closed behind me, and I panted in the corner, sure the entire magical world knew I was defenseless. I'd trapped myself in a box where anything could come get me. Mist could pour in through the crack in the door. Winged monsters could rip open the ceiling and tear me to shreds. The doors dinged back open on my floor, and I squeezed through them before they shimmied apart all the way.

The keys fumbled around in my hands as I tried to find the right one and open the door. They slipped from my fingers and clattered to the floor so loudly it felt like I had just set off an alarm that wailed, *Helpless idiot alone in the hall!*

My heart thudded as I grabbed the keys and jammed the right one into the lock. I leapt into the apartment and flung the door shut behind me.

I leaned against the door, panting. I wanted to lock myself in my room and hide under my bed, but I had rat king blood on my shoes, and I smelled like burnt fur and flesh.

I ripped off my sneakers and risked death opening the apartment door long enough to throw my shoes as far down the hall as my non-athletic self could manage.

"*Nudla.*" I bolted for my bedroom. The spell hissed as it cleaned my clothes, and tingled my scalp as it scrubbed my hair.

I slammed my bedroom door and clicked the lock shut. I

wanted to shower. A nice hot shower to wash away every trace the rat king had ever existed. But what if some unknown evil found me in the shower and I became the worst horror movie cliché?

"*Nudla.*" The spell tingled on my skin.

"*Nudla.*" I crawled up onto my bed, back to the corner, staring at the door.

"*Nudla, Nudla, Nudla.*"

8

I'm not proud of how long I hunched on the corner of my bed trying not to panic, fighting to remember that I wasn't completely helpless without the library in the phone.

After a while I started repeating all the spells I could remember in my head. I got to fifty and started feeling better. I was limited but not helpless. That's when feeling started to come back to my feet and I decided I needed to get to work before Mom got back from school and inevitably reamed me out about the bake sale money.

I pulled out my computer and went to a sketchy text-from-the-web site.

My mom took the phone. At home and grounded. If you need me, you'll have to come to me.

I sent that message to Eric, and the weight on my chest got a little lighter.

Mom took both my phones. Eric thinks there might be something bad coming. Contact him if you need help.

I sent the message to Elizabeth and Devon before sending a shorter message to Elizabeth.

Sorry I left you with the bag. I miss you.

I shut my computer and lay back on my bed. Things were happening too fast. We had spent months working on finding the deformed critters I had accidentally created, and in two days they were all gone. We had been on a long peaceful streak, but now Eric thought it was going to end. Truth be told, I felt it, too. Life was speeding up again, moving more quickly, like something dangerous was chasing us and time was trying to run away.

"I should be training!" I shouted at the ceiling.

Mrs. Mops howled from the living room in response.

I started going through the list of spells I knew again. If there was something coming, we had to be ready this time. I couldn't risk my friends' lives again.

———

"Bryant!" Mom's shout dragged me out of sleep. The sun had gone down, and the only lights left outside were artificial.

I instinctively felt my pockets for my phones. My stomach dropped as I remembered they weren't there. But Mom was home. If I could convince her....

"Bryant Jameson Adams!" Mom shouted. "Out here, now."

"Yes, Mom." Girding my loins, I went out into the living room.

Mom thumped across the room, pacing like a lioness.

"How was the rest of your day?" I tried to sound casual, but my voice got all wavery and gave me away.

"How was the rest of my day?" Mom repeated. "Well, after finding out my son ditched school for not one but two wholly irresponsible reasons, I went to the bake sale my students have been bending over backward to make work so we can try and keep the theatre department running. To try and preserve the thing I have spent the past twelve years building! We go to count the bank, and guess what I find?"

"You made a lot of money?" My voice cracked. That right there was why I could never ever be an actor.

"We made $102,421.54, Bryant." Mom stalked forward, more terrifying than any of the monsters I had ever faced. "How do you think that happened?"

"Really good cookies?"

"How much did your father put in?"

I swallowed hard and spoke as calmly as I could muster. "None."

"Don't you dare lie to me, Bryant. How much?"

"A hundred thousand."

Mom melted down onto the couch.

"He really wants to help with the program." I hurried to sit next to her, hoping to find a window in her moment of weakness. "He wanted to make sure you could rent a space for your performances."

"I used to be able to trust you, Bryant." Her voice sounded hollow, like I'd cracked something inside her. "You were such a good kid. I could trust you to tell the truth. I could count on you to be the responsible one."

"Dad wanted me to take the money. I told him you would know it was him. I said it wasn't a good idea."

"This isn't about the money, Bryant." She rested her head in her hands, looking more exhausted than I had ever seen her. "The last couple of months have been rough. Knowing you're out with Eric kills me. Knowing there are people who want to hurt you destroys me every day. But I thought I could count on you to be where you said you would be, doing what you said you'd be doing. And now I know I can't."

"That's not true, Mom." I shook my head. I could feel the conversation tilting, going in a direction I didn't know how to come back from. "I've been following the rules. It was just today." The lie burned in my mouth.

"It doesn't matter." Mom stood up. "I know you want to be a wizard, but this has gone too far. I'm sorry, but I can't let it continue."

"What?" I sprang to my feet. "I can't just stop being magical. I can't turn it off. That's not how it works."

"What do you want me to say? That I'll let you keep lying to me when I know damn well there are things out there I can't protect you from? The further you dive into magic, the more dangerous it gets. I won't lose my son to a pack of mole people!" Tears streamed down her face.

I hadn't seen my mom cry in forever. I forgot how to breathe.

"Even if I wanted to stop, I can't." I lowered my voice like I was talking to a spooked animal. "It's fate that pulled me into this, and it won't just let me walk away. If something dangerous wants to come for me, it'll come whether I'm working with Eric or not. He's helping me be ready. Eric is teaching me to be safe, to defend myself. Making me stop would make things worse, not better. Please, Mom. I promise I'll be totally honest from now on. But I have to do this."

She stood frozen, staring at me for a long moment. "Then I'll just have to take you far enough away that danger can't find you." She grabbed her purse and coat and headed for the door.

"That's not possible, Mom. You can't run from fate. It'll only make things worse." I sounded like Eric.

Mom rounded on me. "I don't give a damn about fate. All I care about is protecting my son."

"Mom—"

"I'm going to see your father."

"Dad doesn't know about any of this." I ran to the door, leaning against it with all my weight. "You can't tell him about magic. He won't understand."

"He'll have to." Mom glared at me so hard I dropped my hands. She meant it. She was really going to tell Dad, and there was nothing I could do to stop it. "We'll find a safe place for you far away from the city."

Before I could process what she'd said, she disappeared through the door.

I sank to the ground.

I was sixteen. Old enough to make my own choices. But if Dad really wanted me to leave the city, he would just hire men to come take me in the middle of the night.

I could fight them off. But I would have to use magic.

I could run away to Beville, but then I would be leaving my life and my parents behind. Elizabeth and Devon would know how to get to me, but that would be it. No Mom, no Dad.

I couldn't leave magic. It was in my blood. Getting rid of it would be worse than trying to rip out all my veins.

I didn't want to leave my family. They were my...my family.

It was an impossible choice.

In an unusual show of affection, Mrs. Mops banged her head against my thigh, purring effusively.

"You're so lucky you're a cat," I murmured.

I gave the cat a pat on the head, which earned me a deep scratch on the back of my hand.

"You've got nothing on Nutty." I got numbly to my feet and went to my bedroom, closing the door behind me. "*Portundo.*" With a faint rumble, my door disappeared, leaving a smooth patch of wall in its place. At least they wouldn't be able to come get me in my sleep. I'd wait until morning. Try and reason with Mom. If that didn't work, I'd find a way to take back the phone and make a run for it.

I curled up on my bed and stared at my new bit of wall, waiting for sleep to come back for me.

9

W hen the sun had started to rise, Mom woke me up. Not
by shouting this time, but by pounding on the wall.

"I'm up!" I hollered. The words seemed so normal even
though I was screaming them through my magical wall. I didn't
bring my door back until I had dressed and packed my school
bag. I even put on my coat in case I had to trap Dad and ten
henchmen in a spell and make a run for it.

"*Pontunda,*" I said when I ran out of reasons to linger.

My door rumbled back into existence, and, taking a deep
breath, I stepped out into the living room.

"Good God." Dad sat perched on the edge of the couch, eyes
wide with terror as he watched me walk through the newly-
formed door.

"Morning, Dad." I wasn't really sure which was weirder. My
dad knowing I was a wizard, or my dad being in my mom's
apartment. Dad hadn't been in Mom's place since she kicked
him out when I was three.

"I told you, Leo," Mom said from her spot on the floor in
front of the door to the hall.

"How the hell did this happen." Dad's face was sheet white.

Like it wasn't his son Bryant standing in front of him, but just some freaky ghost who'd stolen my face.

"Fate mostly." I stepped into the living room, not letting go of my backpack.

"Fate?" Dad looked from Mom to me. "*Fate* made him able to do this. Fate turned my son all...all..." My dad mouthed like a fish. My dad, who made massive amounts of money talking to super important people, couldn't think of the words to say his son was a wizard.

I didn't know what to say to a man who looked at me like I was possessed, so I stuck to the fate thing. Like if I showed him the big picture first, maybe he would see I wasn't some weirdo. Magic was a huge thing, and the random pull of a golden thread meant I got to be a part of it. And it was awesome.

"Fate sort of has a different meaning with magic," I said. "And I've been—"

"Eric, the man who nearly got him killed, taught him about *fate*," Mom growled.

Mrs. Mops jumped into her lap, kneading Mom's panic sweatpants with her sharp claws. By *panic sweatpants* I mean the pants that meant she was on the edge of insanity and dressing for comfort on the way to the loony bin.

"And what sort of a"—Dad swallowed hard—"wizard are you, son?"

My heart flipped to my ears when Dad said *wizard*.

"A new one," I said. They were both staring at me so hard. "An apprentice, I guess."

"An apprentice." Dad nodded knowingly. I think he was happy it was a word he knew. His big fancy company had apprentices.

"I've learned a lot, but there's a ton more to go." I stepped toward Dad, hoping he would be the reasonable one and understand why what I was doing was so important. "There is a whole world of magic right here in New York, and I've only seen the very tip of it."

"And most of it's in New York?" Dad leaned forward in his seat, like he was leaning over a conference table.

"Well, the Library and The Consortium are here, so this is where magic has sort of congregated, but there's no rule about wizards having to stay here. It's just their home, and they want to stay in it. Magical roots, sort of literally with the shadows." I was rambling. Giving them too much.

"Then there shouldn't be a reason you have to stay in New York." Dad looked to Mom, who brushed Mrs. Mops off her lap but didn't stand.

"Your father and I are very concerned, Bryant. We know you love magic and want to be a part of it. But it scares us both terribly. I know how dangerous it is. I've seen it. It nearly killed me."

"Kate." Dad turned to Mom. Apparently she had left the being trapped in a lifesaving cocoon bit out.

Mom gave a tiny shake of her head.

"Your mother and I love you very much, and we are here because we're concerned for you."

"Is this an intervention?" I laughed harshly. "Are we having a magical intervention right now?"

We'd gone from not being able to say the *w* word to an intervention in a minute. My heart dropped back down to its normal spot and started thumping a panicky rhythm.

"We want you to be safe," Dad pressed on, "and the only way we can do that is to take you out of the city."

"Out of the city?"

Dad nodded. "There are some wonderful boarding schools only a few hours away."

It felt like he'd punched me in the gut. "Your big plan is to ship me off to boarding school?" I rounded on Mom. "You've been fighting to keep me with you in the city for years, and now you cave?"

"Bryant—"

"One afternoon!" I shouted. "I ditched one afternoon of school, which you started!" I pointed a shaking finger at my father. "So now you just want to pack me up and send me away?"

"It's not like that, Bryant." Dad's voice was firm and set, like he was negotiating with someone who didn't want to be bought out. "We're trying to keep you safe."

"I won't be safe! There is nowhere magic can't and won't follow me! The Ladies who almost killed Mom could come after me anytime they want. Shadow people could come after me. Monsters could come after me. And they won't care how far they have to commute to get to me! Running away and pretending I'm not a wizard isn't going to make me any safer. It's only going to make me less prepared!" My chest heaved, and I wanted nothing more than to fling open the door with magic and stomp away. But Mom was still sitting in front of the door.

"If you really think there are people after you, we can send you to school farther away. I have a friend on the board of an excellent school in England." Dad didn't even look sad. He was speaking perfectly calmly about shipping his only child to the other side of the ocean.

"How much did he say he'd give your program?" I spat at Mom. "A million? Two? Enough to rebuild the whole theatre? How much did he offer you to send your son away?"

She looked like I'd slapped her in the face, but I didn't care.

"Don't you dare speak to your mother that way." Dad stood up. He was taller than me, bigger than belonged in our living room.

"Don't pretend you get to make the rules in this house. You just found out about magic today, so don't think for a second you understand any of this." I turned and walked back into my bedroom.

"I understand you're my son." Dad followed me, but I'd already reached my bedroom window. "All I want is what's best for you!"

I rammed open the window. The ill-fitted glass shook in the frame.

"What the hell do you think you're doing?" Dad tried to step around me, but I ducked under his arm, planting my hands on the windowsill.

"I'm going to school." Without looking back I leapt out the window, muttering, "*Escata*," under my parents' screams.

I freefell eleven stories before the air around my legs solidified, turning into invisible pudding that stopped me a few feet above the ground.

"Bryant!" Mom's terrified voice carried down from my window as I pulled one of my feet free and the spell disappeared. I didn't look up. I didn't want to see their faces and wonder if they were more afraid that I had jumped or that I had managed to stop my fall.

I walked out of the tiny courtyard and onto the sidewalks, not stopping until I was around the corner.

There was a lot to process. Too much to process.

My parents wanted to send me away, take me out of the only city I had ever called home.

No way I could let that happen.

I could stay in the city if I stayed away from magic.

I thought for a second about not using magic ever again. About slipping through life day to day without ever uttering another spell. My skin started tingling like every part of my body had fallen asleep at once. I couldn't stop doing magic. It would hurt. I had been warned before, but now I knew without a doubt it was true. And even if I wanted to dodge my magical fate, the

Ladies, and whatever else might want to kill me, Eric, and quite possibly my best friend and girlfriend, would still hunt me down.

That left running away. Getting someplace where my parents couldn't find me and force me onto an airplane.

The look of pure hurt on my mother's face when I'd accused my dad of buying her off flashed in front of my eyes. I shouldn't have said that.

I took a step to go back to the apartment and apologize. But if I went back, we'd fight again.

I screamed, a horrible roar of fear and frustration. The sound echoed off the nearest building, and two women skittered across the street to get away from me.

I'd have to move to Beville. I'd move into the gray stone house with Eric and focus on my training. I might be a high school dropout tomorrow morning, but that was okay, right? Wizards didn't need diplomas, right?

My stomach gurgled as I realized I had a plan. I'd go to school, make it through to lunch. Then I could tell Elizabeth and Devon at the same time. I was going to be leaving the normal world to live with the magical mole people. Then I'd go.

Live belowground. All the time.

A weight pressed on my chest like Manhattan was practicing burying me alive.

Weird thoughts raced through my head as I walked toward school. Would I be allowed to come aboveground to take Elizabeth out on dates? Would I be allowed to get a job to earn money to pay for dates? Was there higher education for wizards? Would I be able to get into my college money to pay for it, or would Dad strip the account?

Every breath seemed like it would rip my chest apart. As I walked up the chipped steps and into school, a black car pulled up in front of the door. I dodged inside and hid behind the doorjamb, waiting for men in fancy suits to come in and grab me. Maybe they'd stick a needle in my neck.

But it was only a steady stream of students coming in through the door.

"Dude, what's your problem?" a senior asked snidely when he caught me peering around the corner.

"Nothing." Sweat pooled on my palms at the lie. I stepped into the oncoming crowd and craned my neck to look at the street.

The black car had parked, and two men stood outside it, their eyes sweeping the crowd.

I let muscle memory carry me to my first class. Devon was waiting, concern showing in his eyes with his first look at me.

"Not now," I said as he opened his mouth. "Wait for Elizabeth."

I couldn't go through explaining everything twice. It was a mark of how good a friend Devon was that he just nodded and didn't ask anything else.

He did keep giving me side-glances during that class and the next. The teachers' voices sounded like they were coming from underwater miles away. They were saying words, but I couldn't hear them. My ears were tuned to much softer sounds. My eyes darted toward the door at every *squeak* of a shoe on the hall floor or *rumble* of distant voices, waiting for Dad's cronies in suits to come drag me away or for Mom to come bursting in in tears.

But nothing happened.

I made it all the way to lunch with nothing at all happening.

10

The space of the cafeteria was overwhelming. Too many people, and too many doors. There was no way to spot where danger might come from.

Elizabeth sat at a table off to one side, an untouched tray in front of her, her eyes locked on me as I approached.

"Come on." Devon patting me on the shoulder nearly made me jump out of my skin.

I yipped like a scared Chihuahua. But no one gawked at me. They were all focused on the lunch line, where the evil lunch lady stood on top of a table, handing out snacks to the crowd.

Elizabeth stood and threw her arms around me as soon as I reached her. "Are you okay?" she whispered in my ear.

"No." That one simple word dissolved all the fight I had left in me. "Dad came to the apartment this morning."

"What?" Elizabeth grabbed my hand and pulled me down to the table.

"Your dad came over to your mom's place?" Devon said.

"Yeah. It was bad. They want to send me away."

"Away?" Elizabeth laced her fingers through mine, and a thrill ran up my arm.

"First, it was boarding school in Upstate, but when I said the Ladies could follow me there, it was England."

"England?" Devon whistled. "Your mom is okay with this?"

"I think it might have been her idea."

"But they can't." Elizabeth shook her head, and her curls swirled around her. "They can't just make you leave."

"They want to keep me safe."

"Are you"—Devon swallowed hard—"are you going to go?"

"He can't. He wouldn't be safe."

"I told them that. And then I jumped out my bedroom window and ran here."

Elizabeth clasped her free hand over her mouth, and Devon swore under his breath.

"You missed the line for treats." The voice made me jump. But it wasn't a giant dude trying to tackle me. It was the evil lunch lady holding out three bright pink cupcakes. "Everyone gets a free treat today."

"What?" It took me a minute to process Her Evilness doing something as nice as offering kids cupcakes. "I'm not hungry, thank you."

"A growing boy your age must be hungry all the time." She smiled, showing overly long teeth. "And a girl as skinny as you needs to put some meat on her bones."

"Meat on my what?" Elizabeth's cheeks got all sucked in like she was literally biting back the urge to scream at the lunch lady about body shaming.

"We aren't hungry," Devon said. "Thanks though."

"I even have gluten-free. I can bring some over."

"No, thanks," Devon snapped.

"Vegan?"

"No."

"Sugar-free?"

"These are great." Devon grabbed the three pink confections and set them on the table. "Thanks a ton."

"You have to try them. I made them special just for you kids."

"Fine." I picked up a cupcake and Devon and Elizabeth followed my lead. I took a giant bite of the surprisingly good treat and smiled. "It's amazing. Thank you for brightening our day."

"Thank you for eating my goodies." She shambled back to her table.

"What are you going to do?" Elizabeth asked as soon as she swallowed her bite and the lunch lady was out of earshot.

"Ask Eric if I can move in with him." I took another bite of cupcake to give myself something to do while they exchanged frightened glances. "I'll understand if you don't want to be a part of any of this anymore. I mean, if you don't want to see a wizard dropout—"

"Don't be a dumbass, Bry." Devon put down his partially consumed cupcake and punched me hard on the shoulder. "You're my best friend. Living in Beville won't change that."

"It'll be like having a boyfriend in Brooklyn." Elizabeth gave a faint smile. "I'll just have to commute to see you."

"I'll miss you." Tears burned in the corners of my eyes. I was so used to seeing them every day. To knowing when I woke up, they were in my near future. I would be giving that up along with everything else. Like sunshine and parents.

"It'll be okay, we'll—"

But I didn't get to hear the end of what Elizabeth was going to say. A *ping* rang through the air, and something like pink pixie dust whooshed up from all the tables.

"Elizabeth!" I shouted over the resounding *bang* as all the doors around me swung shut. "Devon!" They had both crumpled to the floor. Everyone in the lunchroom had crumpled to the floor. "Elizabeth!" I shook her shoulders, but she didn't move. "Help!" I scanned the room, searching for whatever had caused every student in the room to drop.

I expected to see a monster looming over the fallen crowd, or even a sheet of pearl white mist creeping in. But there was nothing but my classmates covered in pink shimmer powder.

"Elizabeth." I bent down to grab her under the arms. I could break open a door, drag her out to the hall, then come back for Devon. But a voice rang out over the cafeteria before I could lift her.

"You must be joking."

I looked up toward the growling voice. The evil lunch lady stood on top of the lunch counter, her steak-like hands on her hips.

"You?"

"Me what?" I stepped over Elizabeth and Devon, planting myself between them and the only other conscious person in the room. "What did you do to them?"

"You ate. I saw you eat." She tipped her head to the side a little too far. Like her neck didn't quite work the same way as mine.

"Did you poison them with glitter?" I took another step forward. "You sick f—"

"Poison is not my ends. Finding the one they're looking for. Collecting the magic one." She twisted her head the other way. "But it shouldn't be you."

"Shouldn't be me? Who the hell did you think it should be?"

Her gaze drifted past me to the floor. Straight to Elizabeth, who lay on the ground, hair shimmering around her like a halo.

Looking at Elizabeth was a mistake. In the second I had glanced away, the lunch lady had grown. Not all of her though. It was like her bones had decided to grow without telling her skin, filling out her wrinkles and sags, making her more frightening than any woman with a hairnet had ever been before.

"No matter." The lunch lady smiled. "They paid for one with magic, and I will deliver. My search led me close enough to find you."

"Who paid you to find me?" I took a slow step to the side, then another. My instinct to stay near Devon and Elizabeth warred with my need to draw the evil lunch lady's attention away from them.

"The ones who want you." She sneered, baring her nasty yellow teeth. "They pay well for fresh ones. How long I've had to look. Waiting and waiting for a fresh one for market. But market day has come, little piggy."

"People are going to eat me!" I halted my sideways progress, too stunned to move. "I don't know which is worse—the thought of being eaten or the irony of a lunch lady searching for human meat."

"Not human." She leapt off the counter, landing ten feet away without a sound. "They pay for magic flesh."

"To eat? I just want to be really clear on that." Her scent of bleach and meatballs reminded me of the importance of escape.

"Not my business what they do once they have you. I only deliver to my master." She smiled. But her lips didn't stop where normal lips should. They stretched back, showing her overly long teeth like an animal preparing to bite. "Best not to fight. They pay more for undamaged goods, and I've waited so long to make a sale. Years and years waiting for one precious item."

"An item for who?" I scooted back toward the front door. It was the largest and had a straight shot toward the main entrance of the school. All my years of plotting for a zombie invasion had finally come in handy. "I mean, if I'm going to be sold, I have a right to know who's doing the buying, don't I?"

"The buyer is not the business of the merchandise." The skeleton lunch lady weaved between tables, snaking her way toward me. Her protruding joints flowed too loosely in their sockets, her knees bending back too far, her fingers flexing like tentacles as they reached for me.

"I find *merchandise* to be an offensive term." I automatically reached into my pocket, my hand searching for the phone that wasn't there. Panic surged in my chest. I didn't have the phone. I didn't even have a way to text Eric and tell him that if I went missing, the six-and-a-half-foot-tall skeleton that used to serve bad pot roast had abducted me.

"You have much larger worries, little wizard." I barely saw her crouch before she sprang at me, flying through the air like a demented grasshopper.

"*Primurgo!*" I screamed the spell, and a shimmering shield appeared around me.

The lunch lady landed on it and smiled at me as she slid down the transparent surface like a kid surfing down a slide.

"Do you want to delay the inevitable, boy? Do you want to fight me?"

In truth, I wanted to scream *no!* and curl up on the floor until the she left, but I knew that wasn't an option. My mind raced, trying to think of something to say, and I spotted Devon's cool black shoes sticking out into the aisle.

Be Devon.

I pulled myself up to stand as straight as I could. "I mean, if you're trying to sell me, I don't think I have a choice but to fight. If you decide you just want to walk away though, I could be feeling generous."

"Cocky little wizard," she growled.

I took cocky as a compliment. It meant I sounded like I wasn't shit-face terrified.

"I don't know who you think you are, but I'm not going with you." I took a swaggering step toward my shield. "I'll give you ten seconds to walk out of this room and never come back. If you don't, there will be consequences." I drew out the word *conse-*

quences like there was some deep, dark meaning I wanted her to understand.

"Consequences?"

"Yeah." I wished Devon and Elizabeth were awake to see me be such a total badass. "I'll have to teach you a lesson."

"If anyone needs a lesson, it's you, wizard boy." In one great leap she flew across the room and landed next to Elizabeth. Lifting her by one limp arm, the lunch lady dangled my girlfriend in the air like a rag doll.

"Don't touch her," I spat as panic squeezed my heart.

Skeletor sneered, and her teeth grew longer and sharper. "Drop the shield, or I kill your girlfriend."

"What?"

"I can rip out her throat. I can paint the floor with her blood. I'd like to see what's in those veins. Such a strong scent of magic on her I couldn't even find you. Magic and death, what has the pretty one been playing with?" She dipped her mouth toward Elizabeth's neck.

"Don't hurt her!"

"Drop the spell, and come with me. No more fighting, no damaged goods, no dead girl."

"Fine." I nodded so hard I thought I would snap my own neck. "Just don't hurt Elizabeth." I released the shield.

With a flick of the wrist the lunch lady threw Elizabeth across the room.

"Elizabeth!" I screamed as she hit the brick wall and crumpled to the ground.

"Oops." The lunch lady cackled, and the laugh shook her whole bony frame.

"If you hurt her, I will kill you." The words weren't even hard to say. They were too true.

"Come with me, or *I* start to kill. And I'm so good at it." The lunch lady took a step that carried her three feet closer to me.

"Which should I start with? The actor?" She pointed to Devon's prone figure on the ground. "The jock?" She pointed to a boy in a football jersey I had never spoken to. A stab of guilt shot through me as I thought how much better it would be if she killed the boy without a name.

"You're not going to kill anyone." I moved backward as quickly as I could without looking down, feeling behind me with my foot for tables and limbs of fellow students. "I'm going to go with you, and I'll take my issues up with your bosses. You're just doing your job."

"And what a wonderful job it is." Her strides were so long she was catching up to me. Soon she would be close enough to grab me. "I could kill just one. To make the job more fun. Make them think the missing boy had lost his mind."

"Are you kidding? They would totally blame the lunch lady." I laughed, hoping I wasn't pushing too far and she would keep talking. "They would say I was a kidnap victim and the lunch lady tried to kill everyone. They'd call me a hero."

"A hero?" The lunch lady kicked one of the band geeks, sending him flying seven feet into the air. "There are no heroes in high school."

"You really need to work on your observation skills if you're going to stalk wizards. I'm starting to think you're not very good at your job." I was three feet from the door, out of reach of all the tables. "I mean, as if the meat loaf weren't enough to prove how incompetent you are."

With a howl, the lunch lady launched herself in the air, flying forward to pounce right on me.

"*Erunca!*" I screamed. A streak of lighting cut through the air striking her mid-leap. The bolt lit up her skin, showing her over-grown bones in sharp relief. I thought she would crumple to the ground, but instead she landed with a stumble and hitch in her breath as though I had punched her.

"I should have killed the girl. I suppose it's not too late," she hissed, twisting to leap back toward Elizabeth.

"*Parapus!*" Thin lines of black flew from my hands and toward the lunch lady like horizontal bars, but before they could *clang* tight around her she batted them aside with her overly long fingers.

"Do you really want to play with me, boy wizard?" She tipped her head too far to the side again. "I don't want to deliver damaged goods. But you give me no choice."

With the tiniest bend of her knees she pounced again, flying through the air so fast I barely had time to throw myself to the ground.

"*Hieata!*"

She gasped and gagged as my spell pummeled the air from her lungs, but she kept moving toward me, step by shuddering step.

I scooted sideways along the wall. She curled a finger in the air, beckoning me forward. I held my breath as she smiled.

One more step. I only needed her to move one more step.

I lunged forward and shouted, "*Abalata!*" A thick band of black sprang from my palm. I threw it as hard as I could, and it stretched like taffy, striking six inches away from the lunch lady's head.

She easily dodged sideways, her eyes dancing with glee, but that move was enough. She was away from the last of the students.

"*Calimarta!*" A great *crack* sounded overhead as a giant chunk of concrete fell from the ceiling.

Fear flashed through the lunch lady's eyes a split second before the chunk hit her with a sickening *squish*. I didn't even have time to want to vomit as blood and squishy body ooze spread across the floor.

"Elizabeth!" I raced to her.

All the people asleep on the cafeteria floor were still, well...
still. The lunch lady's death hadn't released them from whatever
magic she'd used.

"Elizabeth." I knelt next to her, too afraid to move her in case
hitting the wall had done some horrible sort of damage. I
wanted to call Eric and ask him what I should do, but there
wasn't any time. Voices screamed in the hall, and thumping
echoed through the room as someone tried to batter down the
door to the main hallway.

I scrunched up my eyes, trying with everything I had inside
me to focus. "*Concursornio.*" The air around Elizabeth shimmered for a moment, and I held my breath, wishing for her to
wake up with every fiber of my being, hoping I hadn't made a
terrible mistake and made everything worse.

Her perfect, glittery eyes fluttered open, and she gasped. The
most beautiful gasp I had ever heard. She gave an exquisite
cough and sat up. "What happened?" She looked around the
room. "Oh, God." She was on her feet before I could stop her.
"Bryant, what happened?"

With a crack, the hinges around the cafeteria door began to
give way. "No time." I clasped her hand in mine and dragged
her over to Devon who lay crumpled on the floor.
"*Concursornio.*" The instant he stirred I leapt up onto the table.
Closing my eyes, I tried to focus my magic out in every direction, which was really, really hard when the fire sirens started
blaring. "*Concursornio.*" I felt the magic whoosh out of me
harder than it ever had before. My head spun like I'd just
inhaled some weird kind of fume. There was no time to let my
head figure out how to be attached to my neck, so I climbed
unsteadily off the table. Elizabeth wrapped an arm around my
waist as I reached the ground.

"What the hell happened?" Devon asked.

"No time," I whispered as the door banged open.

The football coach and three other teachers tumbled into the room.

"Get out!" I shouted with as much authority as I could. "It's gas! I think there's gas!"

"Everybody out!" the football coach bellowed, lifting two barely-conscious students by the arms and dragging them away.

"We have to get out of here. Now." I grabbed Devon and Elizabeth by the hands and charged to the front of the stumbling crowd, which surged for the door. Everything was still covered in pink, sparkly dust. They wouldn't buy the gas story for long.

"We need help over here!" the English teacher shouted as she tried to shove the concrete chunk off the squished pile of former lunch lady.

Emergency lights flashed in the hall, and everyone charged toward the front door.

"Just keep moving," I spoke as loudly as I dared. "Don't stop for emergency workers or anything. We have to get out of here."

"Bryant!" Mom's panicked voice shot over the sirens as only a theatre person's could. "Bryant!" She raced down the hall toward me. I wanted to dodge out of the way, but there was nowhere to go.

"Are you okay?" Mom took my face in her hands, checking me over for damage.

"I'm fine, but we have to go."

"Let's get you to the ambulances." Mom tried to take my arm, but I shook her off.

"I can't."

People flooded around us, bumping into us as they fled in panic. But the four of us stayed, like a rock in the middle of a creek, immobile in the current.

"Bryant, there was a gas leak." Mom spoke between clenched teeth, hurt and fear showing in her eyes. "You need help. We can figure everything else out later."

"They can't help me, Mom. It wasn't gas, and it's not over yet. I have to go. We all do. Before something else happens to the school, before they find me again."

Mom's hands flew up to her mouth. "Your father has people outside. They can take you away." Tears streamed down her face.

"No they can't. If they found me here, they can find me anywhere."

"He's right, Ms. Miller," Devon said. "I don't even know what's happening, but I know hiding won't work."

Firemen charged down the hall.

"I'll come with you. We'll figure this out."

"You can't." Elizabeth said. "You have to stay here."

"No."

"We need you to make sure no one asks questions about Bryant, or any of us," Devon said. "He needs you to do that. We need you to stay."

"No, please." Tears coursed down Mom's face.

"We have to go. I'm sorry. I love you." The words hurt like a knife twisting in my gut. It didn't matter what had happened that morning. She was still my mom, and I loved her and I had to leave her in a panicked hallway.

Elizabeth squeezed my hand and started down the corridor, trailing Devon and me behind her like kindergarteners playing follow-the-leader. Men ran past, pushing a stretcher.

"Bryant, wait!" Mom lunged at me, throwing her arms around me. "I love you, baby boy."

Two of the men in dark suits my dad had sent came into the hall. I ducked, hiding my face in Mom's shoulder as they passed.

"I have to go," I murmured, pulling painfully away.

"Be safe." Mom pressed something into my hand and ran down the hall toward the cafeteria, shouting to the students, "Everyone get outside! Now!"

I glanced at my hand. The black phone sat in my palm, perfectly smooth and undamaged by its time away from me.

"This way." Elizabeth grabbed me by the arm, dragging Devon along with her other hand. We cut sideways out of the main hall and to the other side of the school.

Wide windows looked out over the sidewalk where students stood, gazing up at the school, some frightened, some disinterested.

Elizabeth hoisted one of the windows open. In one smooth movement she sat on the ledge, twisted to lower herself as far as her arms could reach, and dropped to the ground.

No one on the sidewalk seemed to care. It was sensible—a way to avoid the scrum at the front door. Devon jumped next. The black car had moved farther down the street, making way for the ambulances and fire trucks that had filed in in front of the school.

"Bryant, come on!" Devon hissed up at me, pulling my attention away from the unibrowed man pacing between the fire trucks.

I climbed up on the windowsill and tried to twist around like the others had. But my scrawny arms had had enough. My fingers couldn't hold me, and I crumpled to the frozen sidewalk in a heap.

Devon grabbed me under the arms and lifted me to my feet. Without a word, the three of us ran as fast as our tired and beaten limbs could carry us around the corner and out of sight.

11

The three of us sat scrunched together, panting in the back of the cab. My limbs tingled with fatigue, Devon looked like he was fighting a migraine, and Elizabeth was so pale she looked like Snow White.

"What the hell happened?" Devon whispered as the cabbie sped toward Columbus Circle. It wasn't far. Normally we would have walked. But I wanted to be hidden in the car, to disguise our scent, to run away and hide from more evil lunch ladies trying to kidnap me. Also, sitting felt really good.

"Not now," I whispered back after a long moment.

Devon scowled and shut his eyes.

"Elizabeth, can you text Eric and ask him to meet us at the entrance?" Mom had given me back the magical phone, but not the one that was actually capable of things like calling or texting.

Elizabeth pulled out her phone. A thin dust of pink glitter puffed into the air.

I held my breath, waiting for her to pass out again. But she just coughed and waved it away like it was normal dust.

"What is it?" she asked in a disgusted tone.

My head throbbed trying to make sense of the coma cupcakes. Eric would know. Eric knew everything.

The cab stopped, and I let him run the black credit card my dad had given me. The card went through without trouble. Apparently Dad hadn't cut me off...yet.

We went back down the familiar steps and squirmed through the expected crowd. My eyes scanned every person we passed, making sure they weren't growing into skeletal monsters.

"*Portunda*," I whispered as we reached the bit of wall that led to Beville. For a terrifying moment I thought the wall would stay solid, but the door appeared, and we slipped through, shutting it firmly behind us. "*Portundo*."

We walked quickly down the corridor. It had begun to feel routine. A commute to magic. Now I wanted the walk to go faster, but I didn't know a way to magic the tunnel to be shorter.

"Now can you tell us what happened?" Devon asked as we left the tiled floor and moved into the roughly hewn portion of the tunnel. "I was eating a cupcake, and then I was on the ground covered in fairy dust with a really bad headache."

"The headache was probably me." I ran a hand over my face, trying to work what had happened into an easily explainable order.

"You're admitting to giving people headaches?" Eric spoke dully from the tunnel up ahead. "And here I thought you were only a pain in the—"

"Eric!" I cried, not even caring that he had been making fun of me. "I didn't know what spell to use to wake them up."

"Why did we need waking up?" Elizabeth asked as we reached Eric.

"My question as well." Eric gave us each a hard look before joining our group moving toward Beville.

"It was the lunch lady. The cupcakes she gave everyone had

something in them to knock people out. She was looking for a magic one. She thought Elizabeth was the one, said she could smell magic on her."

"Smell it on me?" Elizabeth shuddered.

"But I was the one who didn't pass out, so she knew it was me. And then her bones got all long and gross, and her teeth grew. She, if you can even be a *she* when you're all demony, said she had waited a long time to find a young wizard and people were going to pay good money for me." I didn't even realize Eric had stopped walking until we were ten feet in front of him. "What?"

"She said people wanted to pay for you?" Eric asked, his face a stone mask.

"Said they would pay more if I was undamaged so I had to come with her nicely. She said"—the words caught in my throat —"she said she would kill Elizabeth if I didn't come with her."

Elizabeth laced her fingers through mine.

"And this lunch lady of yours didn't know you were the one she was looking for?" Eric asked. "She hadn't been sent specifically for you or tracked you by your scent?"

"She smelled magic but thought it was Elizabeth. I told you that." Frustration bubbled in my chest. What was the point in explaining everything if Eric wasn't going to pay attention?

With a muttered curse I didn't understand, Eric charged down the tunnel so quickly the rest of us had to run to catch up.

"What is it?" Devon asked, keeping pace with Eric.

"Worse than what I had hoped for is a descriptive beginning," Eric said, his words coming out evenly as we ran. "I'm afraid what you have just described is a Lancre."

"A what?" I puffed. The end of the tunnel came into view. It felt like we were running with a demon at our heels.

"A Lancre. In the simplest of terms, a witch hunter."

"Like a burning-at-the-stake kind of witch hunter?" Elizabeth asked. "I thought that sort of thing stopped a long time ago."

"It did." We turned onto the street and pelted toward the gray stone house. "But like all occupations, it evolved."

The door to Eric's home sprang open as we charged up the steps. Eric didn't speak again until we were all inside and the bolts had closed with a resounding *thunk.*

"Lancre started off as witch hunters, following one of the greatest haters of our kind that has ever been recorded." Eric led us down the hall toward the parlor. "But as time went on, magic immigrated to the New World, witches became more adept at hiding, and public execution of those accused of witchcraft became a less prevalent form of entertainment."

"Entertainment?" I asked, my legs getting wobbly at the sight of Eric's couch. I collapsed onto the finely upholstered sofa and buried my head in my hands. "Burning witches was entertainment?"

"The hunting, the trials, the executions, it was all for the appeasement of the masses. A way to pass the dark days of the past." With a *crack* the walls shook. I looked up in time to see the bottom half of the room change from wallpaper to packed bookshelves that matched the top half. Eric examined the bottommost shelf as he continued. "When that delightful source of fun ended, the Lancre discovered they had to find real witches to fulfill their pleasures."

"Real witches?" Elizabeth squeaked. "They had been burning fake witches?"

"A person with actual magical ability would be incredibly difficult to restrain and kill. Of course, there were those who were too untrained to fight back or those who chose not to and became martyrs to magic.

"In most cases, however, it was only the unpopular or the too popular who were targeted and killed." Eric pulled an old leather volume from the shelf. The spine was a faded maroon with gold lettering that had flaked away in places. "Once the Lancre were forced to find real witches, they found themselves ill-equipped for the task. Using the magic they so despised, they altered their forms to become monsters like the one you met today."

Eric opened the book and set it on the table at the center of the room for us all to see. I pushed myself to my feet, my legs burning and stinging from even that small effort.

Elizabeth gasped beside me as she looked at the book. It was an illustration of a naked man with bones that had grown too long for his frame and teeth too long for his mouth.

"Dude," Devon whispered.

"Is this what you saw?" Eric asked.

"Yeah." My throat crackled like I'd swallowed sandpaper.

With a *snap* and a *rumble*, the surface of the table shook, and a silver tray with four steaming teacups, a teapot, and a plate of cookies appeared, growing from its surface. Eric snatched the book away just as the teapot would have knocked it from the table.

"So witch haters, who are witches, decided to change themselves with magic so they could trap people with magic more easily?" Devon added sugar to his tea, his hand shaking as he gripped the tiny spoon.

"Would that it were so simple," Eric sighed. "Fighting amongst witches is a time-honored tradition. Lancre are humans. Humans who have bargained with witches to have magical changes made to their bodies but still possess no magic themselves."

"But what about the cupcakes?" I asked, my mouth full of cookie. "They had poison and glitter in them."

"Potions require magical ingredients, not a magical creator," Eric corrected.

"But what witch would give a witch hunter potion ingredients and tracking and fighting skills?" Devon asked. "I mean, doesn't that seem like a terrible idea?"

"A terrible idea can seem brilliant to terrible people," Eric said. "In magically modifying Lancre, they become indebted to you, either constantly as hunting dogs, or let loose in the world with the knowledge that someday you will call upon them to do your bidding."

"That's sick." I hesitated with another cookie halfway to my mouth. Hunger won out over revulsion, and I bit into the gooey treat. Eric's house was a really good cook.

"It is sick." Eric sank back into one of the two winged armchairs, and Devon into the other. "It's even banned by the Ladies. One of their policies I wholeheartedly agree with."

"Okay." Elizabeth took my arm and guided me back to the sofa. "Let me get this straight. Someone broke the laws of the Ladies and created a Lancre?"

"Yes, they can only be created by witches and wizards." Eric sipped his tea, a look of skepticism on his face as though wondering where Elizabeth's thoughts might be heading.

"How illegal is making a Lancre?" Elizabeth asked. Her leg was pressed into mine even though the couch was wide enough for three people to sit. If we hadn't just almost been killed, it might have passed for a lunch date.

Me cozying up to Elizabeth, books all around us, white lace curtains covering the windows. We could make Eric and Devon leave us alone and spend some time kissing on the window seat, holding books in our hands, pretending we might actually read them.

"If you're thinking of asking Bryant or me to make a Lancre, I can assure you it won't happen." Eric ruined my lovely dream by speaking. "If we were to call Bryant's deformed animals a misdemeanor, creating a Lancre is a felony worthy of a life sentence. A Lancre is a thinking, plotting, magically altered being whose sole purpose is to track and destroy witches."

"So whoever made the lunch lady a Lancre must be a fugitive," Elizabeth said.

Eric nodded.

"So a fugitive sent a Lancre after Bryant."

"She thought it was you." I squeezed Elizabeth's hand.

"My best guess is she was told to find a wizard and given a general idea of where to go by her creator. From there she would lay in wait for new witches or wizards to show themselves. Since you and Elizabeth are so closely intertwined, it's not surprising she guessed wrong." Eric pinched the bridge of his nose. "What I want to know is who in New York would be foolhardy enough to set a Lancre loose in the city."

"She worked there for two years," Devon said. "She came halfway through our freshman year. She replaced the lady who gave me extra Jell-O if I winked at her."

"She was in the school before I was a wizard." I took a sip of tea, letting the hot liquid wash away the panic that had been building in my stomach.

"You were always a wizard, you simply hadn't shown any magic," Eric explained. "The scent of magic on you would have been too dull for her to track you specifically, but it would have been clear someone in the school possessed magic."

"Then why did it take her so long to come after me? I've been using magic for months."

"You burned down the theatre with magic." Eric leaned forward in his seat. "Everyone who was touched by those flames smelled like magic to the Lancre. It had to wear off enough for her to smell the continuing magic you three have been party to."

"But why—" Devon began, pointing to Elizabeth, but she cut him off.

"Wouldn't it have been easier to just wait around Beville and snatch someone than to stalk a school for two years?"

"The type that employ Lancre want fresh magic. Newly-formed wizards are what they trade in," Eric said.

My insides squirmed at the thought of being a thing for trade.

"But—" Devon began, huffing loudly when Elizabeth cut across him again.

"So a fugitive who specializes in kidnapping new wizards made a highly illegal magical modification to the lunch lady and laid in wait for years in New York, the heart of modern magic."

"Yes." Eric drew out the word.

"Then we should turn them in to the Ladies." Elizabeth smiled, her eyes dancing with some plan I didn't quite understand.

"The people who tried to kill us right out there on the street?" Devon pointed through the window. It was true. The Ladies had done their best to slaughter the lot of us a few hundred yards from where we sat. "We should just saunter up to The Consortium, knock on the door, and say, *Hey, I think I might have a couple of fugitives for you. But not us. Please don't murder us*?"

"The animals are gone," Elizabeth spoke excitedly. "They were the one thing the Ladies could legally punish us for. We didn't tell them to come to the battle. They can't pin that on us. The only thing they have on any of us is collusion with outside forces"—a really nice way to say Eric worked for a seriously evil dude, but whatever—"and possession of the phone. So we find whoever made the Lancre, turn them over to the Ladies, and ask them to call it even!" Elizabeth finished triumphantly, and the room fell silent.

Devon didn't even bother to slow clap.

"It would be a brilliant plan if the Ladies believed in law and punishment the way you are used to aboveground," Eric said slowly. "And I agree, stopping the maker of the Lancre is of vital importance, not only for Bryant's safety, but for the safety of all in New York. Turning the creator in to the Ladies might even be the wisest plan if we manage to catch them alive."

"But?" Elizabeth asked.

"Turning the creator in would hardly wipe our tarnished slate clean." Eric spread his hands and looked up to the ceiling. "I'm not sure there is a deed in Manhattan that would set our tally right with the Ladies. And if there were, it would be too dark to be done without losing one's soul."

I didn't ask if he meant literal soul or like *I did something that went against everything I believe in* soul.

"Okay, then." Elizabeth growled with frustration. "What do you suggest we do?"

"First, we find the creator and rid Manhattan of the evil of one who trades in new magic," Eric said, "then we go after the Ladies."

"Go after the what?" I yelped at the same moment Devon said much more calmly, "Go after as in *attack*?"

"The magic done at your school is the violation the Ladies have been waiting for. They can now come after Bryant without even needing to publicly mention their embarrassing defeat by Thaden, Charles, and of course, us." Eric bowed to the group. "The Ladies are weaker now than I have ever seen them, but removing an aboveground threat like Bryant would go far in proving their worth to those they rule. Whether by design or by accident, the creator of the Lancre just made Bryant a political target."

12

We talked about plans for a long time. Eric went on and on about how we needed to find the creator and bring them down, then go straight after the Ladies. Devon ranted about how we should go after the Ladies first. Eric said no. Elizabeth said everyone needed to calm down and eat, so we went to the dining room to sit around the shining wooden table, which was big enough to fit twenty people.

The table produced food, we ate, and they argued. I half-tried to keep up. My brain was too foggy to follow their fighting. We had to stop the creator before they made another Lancre to try and grab me or some other poor kid who was new to the magic crazy pot. I got that much.

We had to stop the Ladies who Eric seemed really, really sure were going to take my squishing the former lunch lady as the announcement that it was now open season on Bryant Jameson Adams hunting. I understood stopping the Ladies, too. I didn't want to end up murdered by mist or spending the rest of my life dodging them. And if the Ladies decided killing me was their best play to show they were still in power, it really was them or me.

It was the details that made the humming in my head buzz loudly over their words. We had to wait for daylight. There was a place to go and find answers. Go in the back way and take everything.

They argued around in circles until the three of them seemed to agree on something.

"Bryant, you've been awfully quiet," Eric said as the plates of whatever it was we had been eating dissolved back into the table. "Are you having second thoughts about joining the magical world? If so, I hate to be the one to tell you it's far too late to leave now."

"It's not that." I shook my head, shutting off the buzzing. "I just..." I took a breath and started again. "I get that we have to stop all the bad guys. I even get that fate likes to speed things up when stuff starts to go wrong. But last time we got into a big battle, the fight was coming after us and we really didn't have any choices. We were cornered and desperate and utterly screwed. Now we're picking who we want to go after and how? It just seems impossibly, I don't know...bizarre? Presumptuous with a hint of death wish? How are the four of us supposed to do all this? Are we going to bring Charles and his army of shadows with us?"

"As I've said, we're on our own." Eric didn't sound mad at me for not paying attention to his grand plan. In fact, he sounded more genuinely sympathetic than he had since the time we trapped my mom in a magical cocoon. "We are going to do this carefully, I promise you. With any luck, by this time tomorrow we'll have dealt with the unpleasant creator and be onto the Ladies."

"I really don't think you're helping." Devon rolled his eyes. "Look, Bryant. Like it or not we've become the people who have to stop the bad guys in order to survive. But we're better off this time. We're choosing to go after them. We're more prepared. It's going to make all the difference." Devon sounded so calm and sure I nodded despite the prickles of doubt and dread on the back of my neck.

"We should all get some rest." Eric stood. "There are plenty of rooms upstairs. The house will lead you where you need to go."

Elizabeth, Devon, and I headed to the shining wooden door that led to the hall. All the doors around us swung open like gleeful tormentors waiting for us to run the gauntlet. None of us had the energy to run as the doors slammed one after the other, *guiding* us up the stairs and into a hall none of us had ever entered before. The slamming of the doors kept chasing us down a corridor far too long to fit in the house, until we reached the end where three doors stayed open. I peeked into the first door. A large canopy bed with ruby-red hangings sat in the center of the room, looking warm and inviting.

"Ladies first." Devon bowed Elizabeth into the room. With a murmured goodnight, she closed the door and was gone.

I didn't like her being out of sight. It was too hard. The memory of her being flung at the wall by an evil, witch-hunting Lancre made me want to tear down the door just to see her safe and sound.

"Come on." Devon pulled me through the next open door. This room was different than Elizabeth's but just as Victorian and fancy. A white iron bedframe with flowery sheets took up the center of the room, and a scent like lavender filled the air. A painting of a castle hung on the wall next to a wide-set wardrobe that looked like it might lead to another world.

"Are you okay, Bryant?" Devon asked as soon as the door clicked shut behind us.

"Oh, yeah," I said a little too enthusiastically. "Just excited for all the dangerous adventuring we have coming up."

"I really want to punch Eric in his stupid wizard face." Devon slid down the wall by the door. "He talks like this is no big deal."

"I think the near-death thing is normal to him." I sank onto the bed. The metal frame creaked and groaned, protesting my weight.

"Normal for him isn't normal for us. We should be at home right now. I should be listening to my dad lecture me on how I need to find a nice girl like my friend Bryant did."

"Your dad says that?" I slid off the bed to sit eye level with Devon.

"All the time, dude." Devon nodded tiredly. "You're like his hero. You were even before Elizabeth."

"Wow." We sat in silence for a moment, like only best friends can. "You could go home, you know. You aren't the one the Lancre sniffed, so you probably don't smell any more magical than everyone else who got pixie-dusted today."

"I'm not going home. I'm not leaving you or Elizabeth. I may not like the idea of trying to take on two bad guys in the next few days, but if that's where you're going, it's where I'm going. I couldn't live with myself if I didn't. Better to fight than be the asshole who abandons his friends." Devon gave a tired grin. "Besides, I texted my parents while we were in the cab and told them I had things to do and wouldn't be home for a while. They've probably thrown all my stuff out the window and shunned me by now."

I returned Devon's smile like I thought it was a joke, even though we both knew he was mostly serious.

That was the problem with being Devon's best friend. I knew his parents weren't great, and I was duty-bound to never mention it. I wasn't allowed to ask why his parents always seemed to be relieved when he left the house or why once every third month they'd freak out if he was ten minutes late when they didn't want him around anyway, and he wasn't allowed to ask why I was terrified of anyone finding out my dad was super rich. It was how we survived.

"Remember when being a hero meant being the one to volunteer to climb the sketchy fire escape to rescue a ball? I miss that." Devon laughed. I think it was the saddest laugh I'd ever heard. "See you in the morning." Devon stood and walked out the door before I could think of something meaningful to say.

"Goodnight," I said to the woodgrain on the door.

I crawled back onto the bed and under the flowery quilt. I missed my bed. Not the one in the linoleum place. The one that had gotten blown up when I ruined my mom's old apartment.

I shut my eyes tight, trying to pretend I was back in the bedroom I had grown up in. Soon Mrs. Mops would come stick her butt in my face and dig her needle-like claws into my chest just to mess with me one more time before I fell asleep.

But a tap on the door came instead of vicious claws.

"Bryant?" Elizabeth's voice drifted through the door.

"Come in?" I said it with a question at the end. Like I was asking if it was all right for her to come in. Mostly because I wasn't sure if it was all right for her to come in.

But Elizabeth slipped through the door without any magical siren blaring, shouting to the world there was a girl in Bryant Jameson Adam's bedroom.

"How are you?" Elizabeth perched at the foot of the bed. Like it was normal for the two of us to be on a bed together.

"*Immummm.*" I'd lost my ability to say words. Two months of dating and now I had suddenly reverted to not being able to speak in front of Elizabeth.

"So about as well as me then."

I crawled over the squeaky mattress and wrapped my arm around her. She was shaking even though it wasn't cold.

"We'll make it through this, you know," I said with as much

determination as I could muster. "It's going to be crazy, but we can do it."

"I know." Tears sparkled on Elizabeth's face.

"What's wrong?" The sight of her silently crying stabbed me right through the heart.

"I'm just"—Elizabeth took a shuddering breath—"I'm so tired. It's been months of this, and now we have to fight again. I just want to rest. Just for a while."

"It's been quiet for two months."

Elizabeth bit her bottom lip, the way she did in math class when she was trying to figure out calculus.

"Unless it hasn't been and you haven't been telling me." I paused for a moment, waiting for her to argue that of course I knew everything and she really just needed a nap.

But she just looked at me with tears in her eyes.

"What haven't you been telling me?"

"A lot," Elizabeth said. "I've been doing a lot."

I waited for her to keep talking, but she just stared at me, like she was stuck between scared and too exhausted to talk.

"Is that why Lola's homeless child guard sniffed me and Eric told him I knew you?" I said.

Shock flickered through Elizabeth's eyes before she nodded. "He's the one who keeps me safe at night. When I'm wandering around, studying the shadows. He's my guard dog."

"But you said he was terrifying. You said they looked like decaying man dogs." The thought of my girlfriend walking around Manhattan with nothing but a dead demon dog for company was horrifying.

"He does." Elizabeth shuddered. "But he keeps me safe. And he can find just about anything."

"You should have told me." I took both Elizabeth's hands in mine. "I could have gone with you. Given you someone alive to talk to."

"It wouldn't be allowed." Elizabeth shook her head, sending her hair cascading around her shoulders. "No non-seers allowed in training."

"Training? I thought you were just keeping an eye on things."

Elizabeth laughed. It started like a tiny giggle, but soon she was laughing so hard I was sure Devon would hear.

"Keeping an eye on things?" Elizabeth finally gasped. "How am I supposed to do that without training? I see creepy things in the shadows, but I can't always tell what they are. I know the shadows swirl by Pearl and Water Street, and not all the people are people in Bowling Green. But how would I know what I was looking at without training? Eric's library has given me some things to study, but it wasn't enough."

"Then how have you been learning?" I glanced stupidly at the door like Elizabeth's teacher would come charging in right on cue to introduce herself.

"Lola, mostly."

I breathed a sigh of relief. Eric's paramour had saved my mom. She was an amazing and powerful seer, even if she did live in exile under a bridge.

"She's been sending me out into the city with the boy, and he's been helping me track things. Different kinds of shadows so I could see them for myself, a few kinds of creatures normal people can't see, sometimes wizards who are trying to hide from the Ladies. Bad things don't always hide in nice places."

"Why didn't you tell me?" I tried to keep the hurt out of my voice. It wasn't like she was seeing another guy, but it still stung.

"I did, mostly." Elizabeth shrugged. "And I didn't want you to worry. You have your own training to think about, you can't waste time chasing after me."

"You aren't a waste of time." I took Elizabeth's face in my hands. "Nothing about you will ever be a waste of time."

"But it is." Elizabeth took a shaky breath. "I'm barely a seer.

I'm not a wizard. I'm only talented enough to be able to tell evil things are coming. I can feel this darkness building and the patterns in the shadows are different, but I don't know what any of it means."

"What sort of evil things are coming?" I asked like a stupidly moronic idiot.

"I just told you, I don't know!" Elizabeth half-shouted, pulling away from me.

"I'm sorry, you did." I held out my hand to Elizabeth, waiting for her to take it. "You can see things I can't even imagine."

"It's like trying to read a language I don't understand. That uses an alphabet I don't know." Elizabeth wound her fingers through mine. "I can tell things are getting angrier and more frightened. Violent sometimes. But I don't know why. And knowing that I don't know makes it worse."

I scooted over to her, pulling her to my chest. She nestled her head on my collarbone. It was the most wonderful and terrifying feeling at the same time.

Elizabeth was there in my arms. The most perfect creation in the entire world wanted me to hold her. But that made it my job to protect her. To keep her safe from whatever might be lurking in the shadows I couldn't even see. The urge to take her hand and run back up to the city, find an airplane, and fly to the other side of the world surged through me. It didn't matter how far we had to run, or how long we had to hide, as long as I could keep Elizabeth safe.

Nothing mattered but keeping Elizabeth safe.

But the Lancre had found Elizabeth's scent, not mine. Even if I could convince Elizabeth to move to Thailand to live on an elephant sanctuary, she still wouldn't be safe.

"Is that why the Lancre scented you?" I asked, still holding Elizabeth tightly. "Because you've been spending so much time with the shadows?"

"No idea." Elizabeth gave a faint laugh. "I'm a seer, not a scenter."

"If you figure it out, will you tell me?" I pressed my lips to Elizabeth's hair, reveling in her scent of fresh flowers with no detectable magic mixed in. "Tell me everything. Because it is all important." I scooted back enough to be able to look into her eyes. "You are important."

"I just"—she gave a shaky sigh—"I didn't want to bother you. With everything you need to learn, and how hard you've been trying—"

I didn't let her finish. I leaned in and kissed her instead. And Lancre didn't matter, and shadows didn't matter, and leaving my parents didn't matter. There was only me and Elizabeth.

13

I would love to say I was super cool and when Elizabeth curled up with her head on my shoulder I totally slept super peacefully like I was finally complete and everything was right in the world. But I didn't sleep. Not really.

I'd drift off for a few minutes, then wake up suddenly, expecting my mom to come into the room screaming at me for falling asleep with a girl. Once I was awake enough to know my mom was definitely not going to come storming into Eric's house since she had no idea how to get to Beville, let alone which house Eric lived in, I'd fall back asleep. Then I'd wake up thinking Eric was going to come barging in with some coy remark about the follies of youth. Then I'd drift off again and think shadows were coming to steal Elizabeth away from me.

But Elizabeth slept, her breathing steady and her beautiful face calm. She slept through each of my mini freak-outs without so much as a murmur. Like she hadn't slept properly in months. Which might have been true. Which made me a terrible boyfriend for not noticing.

The cycle continued until the house decided it was time for us to wake up. The lights in the room all flicked on at the same moment the wardrobe doors gave a bang that would have shattered any normal glass.

With a scream, Elizabeth tumbled off the bed, hitting the floor with a shriek and a *thud*, while I leapt to my feet, standing on the bed and screaming, "*Primurgo!*"

The shield blossomed around the bed, but only the wardrobe moved. Its doors swung open to show a set of perfectly pressed clothes as the door to the hall flew open.

"Is that my cue to go?" Elizabeth whispered. The door opened wider in response. "Okay then." Elizabeth stood silently and crept out into the hall. As soon as she passed the threshold the door slammed shut behind her.

"Thanks." I rolled my eyes at the door.

The knob rattled in response.

"Though I don't see why you should care where Elizabeth sleeps." Heat flooded my face just talking to the house about Elizabeth sleeping in my room. I'm not sure how to explain it, but I swear I could feel the house judging me.

I headed for the door to the hall, but a barely visible narrow door behind the wardrobe swung open with a *creak*.

"What?"

The door opened a bit wider.

"Fine."

The door didn't lead anywhere dark or dangerous. Just to a bathroom with white and blue tiles. The scent of strong soap filled the air. The fancy carved showerhead hovering over the claw foot tub turned on as I stepped into the room.

"So now you're telling me I smell?"

Instant food delivery was great, and having a house that wanted to keep you alive during a battle also had some definite pluses. But when the house gets all judgey and tells you to bathe, it gets a little weird.

Not weird enough for me to refuse a hot shower, though. I

mean, I had been covered in rat king blood and pixie dust, fought a Lancre, and run for my life since my last shower.

I didn't suspect anything until I climbed back out of the shower and reached for my pile of clothes on the floor. My fingers met nothing but smooth, cool tile. "Aww, come on!"

I ran into the bedroom, chasing the vain hope that maybe my clothes would be magically clean and folded on the bed. My hopes were smashed as soon as I got into the room. The bed was perfectly made, and my clothes were nowhere in sight.

"No, no, no," I groaned, turning to the wardrobe.

The doors gave a joyful little wiggle on their hinges, happily displaying the neatly hung clothes.

"I could just decide to go naked, you know!"

If a wardrobe could laugh I swear this one would have. Luckily, there were no enchanted roses to be had in this house, so the doors just wobbled a bit harder.

"Fine!" I yanked the clothes from the hanger. "You want me to wear a suit, fine!" Socks and underwear tumbled out of the dresser, landing at my feet. "Oh, how very kind of you."

I didn't look in the mirror as I pulled on the suit. The house was making me dress like Eric's mini-me. A black, three-piece suit with a white dress shirt, fancy black shoes that really didn't seem suited to running for my life, and even a black bowtie to cap off the turn-of-the-century horror. I snatched up the black bowtie. It wasn't even a clip-on. I had a horrible feeling that if I held the tie up to my throat it would tighten for me.

"Nope, that's too far." I threw the bowtie back onto the bed. "I draw the line at bowties."

Storming over to the door, I half-expected the knob not to turn until I completed the macabre ensemble. But the door opened easily, and I darted into the hall before the house had a chance to change its mind.

"Elizabeth? Devon?" I called, waiting dumbly in the hallway. It only took a moment for Devon to pop his head out his door.

His eyes traveled up and down my outfit before he bit his lips together to pinch back a laugh. "And here I thought I was the only one the house decided to mess with." Devon stepped out into the hall. He was dressed in an all-black suit that looked like it belonged on a billboard. He didn't have a white shirt with a dodgy collar. He had a fancy, black, collarless shirt with no place for a tie. I looked like an undertaker—he looked like an international spy. Sometimes having a super cool best friend sucks.

"You boys look nice." Elizabeth stood behind us smiling, looking like a time-traveling angel. She was wearing a 40s-style dress, like the ones my mom used for *Guys and Dolls* when the costumer couldn't find anything decade-appropriate for the show. It was all black with thin, white trim tracing a line around her neck and down the long rows of buttons in the front. Black stockings and lace-up heels completed the look of perfection.

"Wow," I breathed, blushing all the way down to my rebelliously unbuttoned collar. "You look...wow."

"You boys look pretty dapper yourselves." Elizabeth's heels clicked on the floor as she walked over and kissed me.

Time stood still. Angelic perfection, kissing me.

"Whoa." Devon coughed. "Get a room." He kept coughing. "But you already did."

Elizabeth pulled away from me and smacked Devon hard on the arm. "Rude." Threading her fingers through mine, she led me back down the overly long hall toward the stairs. Devon followed behind, snickering at us.

"Breakfast in the parlor or dining room?" Elizabeth asked loudly as we reached the bottom of the stairs.

The doors on one side of the hall swung open and banged shut, ushering us toward the parlor.

"Thanks," I muttered to the house, not feeling really friendly toward the judgmental building who had made my friends look cool and me look like a stooge.

The smell of freshly baked bread wafted out of the parlor. Eric sat in one of the two large armchairs, balancing a teacup in one hand and a croissant in the other. Mouth watering, I headed straight toward the round table, grabbing a pastry and shoving it into my mouth.

"How very delicate of you, Bryant," Eric said dryly. "Though I suppose an elegant exterior can't immediately change the interior."

"Elegant?" I choked through my mouth full of food. "I look like a pallbearer."

"No one would have you as a pallbearer." Eric stood and batted my hand holding the rest of my croissant away from my mouth. "You've forgotten the tie. You look like a cretin with your top button undone."

"He looks dashing." Elizabeth smiled coyly as she poured herself a cup of tea.

"I'm not wearing the tie." I took a defiant bite. "And you can't make me." I finished with my mouth mostly full.

Eric gave a disgusted sneer. "After we've worked on your table manners, we can begin on the attributes of proper dress. You need to be taught bowties are cool."

"And why do we need cool new duds?" Devon asked as he settled into the other armchair. "Are we going for a trip to the country club?"

"Surprisingly correct." Eric nodded to Devon before pouring himself another cup of tea.

"Correct how?" I asked after the pause in explanation lasted long enough for Eric to pour the tea, add sugar and cream, and sit back down in his chair.

"While you lovely children—"

"Offensive, man," Devon inserted.

"While you younglings were sleeping blissfully, I was doing a bit of digging," Eric finished.

"What sort of digging?" Elizabeth leaned so far forward off the couch I thought she might fall.

"The sort of digging our lovely seer wouldn't be suited for. There are rumors in the city of a new dark wizard. One who fancies himself above the law. This prince of discord has been bold enough to set up his kingdom aboveground, and clever enough to keep his name out of the shadows."

"And he sent the Lancre?" I sank down onto the couch next to Elizabeth.

"Presumably." Eric took a slow sip of his tea. "I don't believe it was anyone who resides in Beville. I whispered to the shadows last night, and they've seen no trace of that kind of magic. It wouldn't be the Ladies. They can scent magic without the foulness of creating a Lancre."

"So this new guy is our only option?" I asked. "I mean, couldn't there be more than one rogue wizard who doesn't live in Beville?"

"Absolutely." Eric raised his cup to me. "I'm sure there might be dozens. But this wizard seems to have a taste for recruiting young talent. He's even lured a few children out of Beville with promises of magic aboveground."

"Does he deliver on those promises?" I asked. A shiver ran down my spine. I leapt up, way faster than the situation warranted, and began making myself a cup of tea, clanking the sugar spoon too hard against the cup.

"Please don't break the china, Bryant," Eric said.

"I mean, does he actually have some wonderful world waiting for the people he steals?" My hands shook as I took a sip of my overly sweet tea.

"I think *recruits* would be a more descriptive term than *steals,* at least for those he's convinced to leave Beville. But as for a wonderful world in the light, I truly don't know." A little wrinkle creased Eric's pale, white skin between his coal black eyebrows.

Eric saying *I don't know* was terrifying. He was always so annoyingly sure of everything. Him not knowing something was like a doctor telling you they didn't really know if you had cancer or not.

"But I doubt it," Eric said. "If he truly had something spectacular to offer, his discreet recruiting would have taken more from Beville, and the use of Lancre would be unnecessary."

"So he takes these kids and does what with them?" Devon asked.

"I have no idea, but that is what I intend to find out. We'll go to this prince aboveground, find out if he did, in fact, send the Lancre to lurk in your school, make sure none in his care are being harmed, and if he is guilty on either of those counts, we will ensure he can never hurt anyone again." Eric set his cup on the table and stood.

"Now?" I asked, my voice trembling enough to have all three of them look at me. "I mean, it's morning. Shouldn't we wait until afternoon?"

"Usually I would agree that a visit before noon is rude, but when seeking one's enemies, the rules of propriety can be set aside."

"So...now, then." Elizabeth grabbed my elbow and hauled me to my feet.

"Once you know where an enemy is, it's best to strike immediately before fate thinks you're lazy and decides to ruin your plans."

"Right." I grabbed an extra croissant and followed Eric out the door.

"You still haven't explained the suits," Devon said as he followed the funeral train down the hall.

"Where we're going, it would be best not to be seen as *other*." Eric stopped by the front door, pulling his long coat off a hook I'd never noticed before. Three other coats hung next to it. He swept a hand for us to take them. "While in your society blending in might be possible with loud and poorly made clothes, this is the camouflage of magic."

I grabbed a coat from the wall, hoping maybe I had gotten the cooler one this time. Nope. Devon looked like he was going to battle inside a computer, Elizabeth looked like a Kennedy, I looked like an asshat.

I slouched out of the house after Eric, doomed to be the dorky sidekick to the suave hero. Elizabeth slipped her hand into mine, and a warm glow started right in the center of my heart, burning away the icy cold jealousy. So I stopped pouting and puffed up my chest. If I was going to be a funeral director, at least I was a funeral director holding the hand of the most beautiful girl in the world.

"What?" Elizabeth asked, giving me a sideways smile as we entered the tunnel to Columbus Circle.

"Nothing." I grinned like the idiot I am. "You just look truly beautiful."

14

I really thought I would get a bunch of weird stares or at least some blatant avoidance on the subway for looking like a harbinger of death. But no one seemed to notice my undertaker-chic ensemble as we took the train to the lower east side.

"Where exactly are we going?" I whispered as another hundred tourists got off of the train, heading for Christmas merriment aboveground.

"You'll see when we get there." Eric smiled as he spoke.

I didn't trust that smile. "What do you mean, I'll see? Are we going to the Empire State Building? Please don't tell me magical forces have taken over the Empire State Building."

"Don't be foolish." Eric chuckled. "The Empire State Building hasn't been in magical hands for the last decade."

"Right. Who doesn't know that?" I leaned back in my subway seat.

"And here we go." Eric popped to his feet as the train rumbled to a stop.

"Allons-y!" Devon bowed, letting Elizabeth and me leave the train first.

A man in a bright red jacket leaned casually against the pole right outside our train door. I searched his face for signs of magic. Not that I knew what a sign of magic would be other than color impairment. But Eric walked past the red coat and headed toward the kiosk on the side. I searched the stand for a door to an enclave of magic, but Eric walked past that, too.

I kept searching everything we passed for a sign of something magical. The stairs leading up to the street didn't turn into a slide to a forbidden underworld. The crosswalk sign wasn't blinking a secret message.

Maybe that dog trying to eat his own leash was the doorman for the secret society of magical kidnappers. Or that old man gumming chestnuts was actually the wizard we were looking for.

"How do you do it?" I whispered to Elizabeth. "How do you see magical things all the time? And spend nights looking for creepy shadows?"

"It's exhausting." Elizabeth sighed, not seeming to think there was anything weird about the little girl having a tantrum and pounding her fists against a frostbitten tree.

The crowds got thicker as we moved toward the more touristy streets. Soon, we reached a scrum that blocked the whole sidewalk.

"Just great," Devon grumbled, cutting out onto the street.

Eric grabbed his arm. "If you want to be in on the fun, you'd best stay here. We've arrived."

I looked up at the building all the tourists had jammed themselves in front of. A giant black-and-white mock vintage sign hung out front.

The Game.

"You have got to be kidding me." A laugh bubbled out of me before I could swallow it.

"Not in the least." Eric stared at me with one eyebrow arched high.

"This is it?" I asked through my torrent of laughter.

"Shhh," Elizabeth hushed as a harassed woman with three whining children turned to glare at me.

"The most popular tourist restaurant outside Times Square is where the kidnapping prince of magic hangs out?" I whispered.

"It's an excellent cover when you consider it." Eric spoke so softly Devon, Elizabeth, and I had to lean in to hear him. "A noisy place known for odd goings-on. The expectation of strangers coming and going."

"A liquor license," Devon added.

"Crass but undeniably true," Eric conceded.

"So what do we do now?" I scanned the crowd. The throng pressed toward a man holding a tablet at the door. All I could see of him over the crowd was a wide top hat and lips pinched with impatience as people complained about the long wait for a table.

"And why is everyone here to eat now?" Devon growled as a tourist stepped on his toe. "Why are you pushing in line to eat now?" he snapped at the offender.

"I don't want to get stuck in line waiting for dinner," the woman coughed in her gravelly, smoker voice.

"Lovely." Eric faced the door and muttered something under his breath.

The crowd parted gently in front of him, like an invisible wedge was plowing subtly through the mass of hangry people. Like Eric was Moses parting the red and green tourist sea.

I trailed in Eric's wake, keeping Elizabeth's hand clasped firmly in mine.

"We'd like a table for four," Eric said as we reached the man.

I forgot to be intimidated as the doorman surveyed us. I was too busy gawking at his outfit, which suddenly made mine feel subtle and chic.

Aside from the wide, black top hat, he wore a deep purple tailcoat to go with his ruffle-fronted shirt. His black leather boots came up to his knees, mostly covering his emerald green pants. He looked like a combination of a horseback rider and a court jester. The illusion was ruined as soon as he spoke.

"There's a wait." His tone was dry and low with a touch of menace. "It'll be about two hours before I have seating for you. You can wait on the street. We don't hold tables."

"A true pity that a magical place such as this is so lacking in customer service." Eric smiled calmly. "I suppose it's quite lucky for us we aren't here for one of the standard tables. We're here to dine with the proprietor."

With a fancy little flick of his wrist, Eric produced a black business card with shimmering gold letters that read *Eric Deldridge ~ Resident of Beville.*

The doorman looked down at the card for a moment, and then with another flick of Eric's wrist, it was gone.

"Just because you've found the place doesn't mean you're the type for entry to the private game," the doorman said.

"Oh, but we are." Eric took Devon by the shoulders and moved him to the front of our group. "I believe I can offer just the sort of merchandise that is of value in the private game."

The muscles on the back of Devon's neck tensed as the doorman looked him up and down as though examining a chunk of meat at a high-end butcher.

"Fourth floor. If you can't open the door, it isn't my problem." He stepped aside, bowing us in.

Eric reached for the handle, but before he could touch the knob, the doorman slammed his hand against it.

"One more thing." The doorman smiled, which was way scarier than his scowling had been. "Play The Game at your own risk."

"Of course." Eric grinned back.

If I didn't know Eric, I might have missed the *I might kill you later* glint in his eyes. Eric pulled open the door, and the crowd roared in protest.

The shouts of "We've been here for an hour!" "You said there were no reservations!" and "I slipped you a fifty!" fell silent as we entered The Game.

The hall in front of us was taken up by a wide, wooden staircase. To the right was a huge archway that opened into a bar, which, despite the early hour, was packed. Not that I'd had much experience in bars, but I knew right away why this one was in such high demand. Bartenders in pointy hats and long robes stirred smoking drinks with the tips of their wands.

Mounted animal heads hung over the roaring fire in the wide brick fireplace. And these weren't the average buck heads of normal creepy hunting cabins. They were mounted magical creatures. Or at least dead things that had been doctored to look like magical creatures. A face of something between a pig and a horse took the center space, flanked by an eight-legged ferret and a bright silver-and-purple bird with a florescent blue beak.

"This is what they think of us." Eric shook his head, sighing heavily. "Better that than the truth."

"The truth?" I asked as sparks flew out of the barback's wand, lighting the sconces around the room to thundering applause from the guests.

Eric rolled his eyes so hard I thought they might fall out. "This way."

We started up the wide, wooden staircase that wrapped around a fancy metal elevator.

"Better to think magic is something from a far removed world utterly beyond normal reach than a specter waiting for you to take one wrong turn," Eric said in a hushed tone.

"Hey," Devon said, "calling Bryant a specter is offensive.

Almost as offensive as calling me merchandise. What the hell was that about anyway?"

"Having something to offer to the private game not only gained us entry into this vulgar place, it also gave us some very important information," Eric said as we made it to the second floor.

"Like what?" Devon asked.

"Like this is a place where a kidnapped teenager would be a hot commodity," Elizabeth said as we rounded the corner and the second floor dining room came into view.

Lights flashed in one corner as a man strapped to a wall writhed, screaming in pain. For a spilt second I thought the tortured guy was a teen stolen by a Lancre, living the horrible fate I had narrowly avoided. But then I saw the vaguely disinterested expression on his face as he screamed.

"He's an actor," I whispered to Elizabeth.

"A bad one," she murmured back as the man broke free of his bindings and stumbled forward into the dining room, lurching toward a group of high school girls who screamed like banshees.

As the man raised his hands toward a girl's throat, another actor burst through a curtain onto a balcony halfway up the wall bellowing, "Halt, my monstrous creation!"

The crowd cheered. I snickered.

"I did not intend to create a beast without a soul!" Balcony guy clutched his chest in mock heartbreak. "Now I must destroy my creation!"

Eric took my elbow, dragging me away from the floorshow and up the next flight of stairs.

A monstrous roar followed us up the steps. If I weren't so used to magic, I might not have noticed how the scream faded too quickly, like a spell had blocked sound from traveling between floors.

"What the hell is this place?" Devon said. "I mean, what kind of tourist lines up for this?"

"The ones who..." I lost the ability to speak as we made it to the third floor.

A man in a red uniform screamed as a light saber slashed through his stomach.

"What?" I shouted. "That's not right!"

"Bryant." Elizabeth tugged on my hand as, with a display of glitter and strobe lights, an android appeared in the wall.

"I cannot feel fear," the pale-faced android said. A gold droid toddled out to the center of the room, bowing to the pale android as Elizabeth yanked me out of sight.

"They can't do that!" I tried to get back to the door as the sounds of laser guns and *wooming* sword slices cut through the air. "That is cross-geek contamination!"

"I'm sorry if this place offends your nerd sensibilities," Eric said from the foot of the last staircase. "I promise as soon as we finish our business here, we can leave this place and its misplaced fandom forever."

"Misplaced fandom?" Devon spread his arms wide. "This place embodies a full range of awesomeness!"

Eric turned on the stairs so quickly Devon ran into him. "I didn't take you for one to indulge in things that weren't bound to attract women."

"I'm more than just a pretty face." Devon stepped around Eric to take the lead. "I have depths you know nothing about."

"Delightful," Eric said dryly as Devon stopped in front of a white-and-black checkered door.

15

The heavy metal door, without a window or doorknob to mar the chessboard design, blocked the top of the staircase.

"Well, Mister Depths-beyond-my-understanding, unless you've suddenly become learned in the magical arts, perhaps you could step aside," Eric said.

Devon growled as they switched places on the narrow stairs.

"Do you think it's a puzzle?" I asked in a stage whisper. The terrible feeling of being watched had goose bumps sprouting all over my neck.

"Perhaps." Eric ran a hand around the edge of the door. "Though I doubt it. This is a place of profit with a customer base of wizards who don't mind breaking the law. Making entry too difficult would be bad for business."

"But keep a better clientele." Elizabeth squeezed past Devon and me, squinting at the door.

"Anything of interest?" Eric moved his fingers between squares like they were doing some strange minuscule version of hopscotch.

"Not that I can see." Elizabeth tipped her head to the side.

"Well then, let us try for the obvious solution. *Cliaxo.*"

A deep *thunk* sounded within the door.

"And simple it is." Eric grinned and pressed on the metal. The chessboard surface swung slowly and silently. It wasn't until it was about halfway open that the thump of music carried out to the staircase. "Shall we?"

Eric didn't spare a glance to see if we were following. He was back in his element. Like the last two months of training had just been a hiatus from his real life of danger and sneaking up on people.

"In we go," Devon murmured, following Eric up the steps.

It was my turn to say something brave and/or cocky. My mind was suddenly blank as I turned to Elizabeth.

Say something cool, Bryant. Just one cool word!

"I've always liked chess." The words fell out of my mouth as involuntarily as vomit.

"Maybe we'll play sometime." Still holding my nonsensical and unworthy hand, Elizabeth climbed the last few steps with me.

For a moment, I thought there was some magical trick messing with my head. The black and white door had expanded into a room. Then I blinked a few times and realized the door was still swung open where it belonged—it was the checker-board pattern that had eaten the room.

The floor was laid out in black and white squares. Unlike the rooms below that were crowded with tables, the center of this floor was almost entirely open. Edged along the walls were black and white booths made of fancy leather, which looked so soft I wanted to curl up and sleep on them.

The only real table in the room sat opposite the door we had just entered. A round, white marble table just big enough to seat four. Two white and two black chairs surrounded it. One of the chairs was filled. By the time my head managed to make enough sense of the room to notice the person staring at us, he'd already stood.

The man had bright white hair spiked into a Mohawk with black tips. His eyebrows and lips looked like he had painted them on with charcoal. But it was his cloak that made me cough a badly-hidden laugh. Black fuzzy fur piled high at his shoulders, like he thought winter was coming, and not in the Manhattan trench coat kind of way. Below the fluffy shoulder pads, a stitched insignia tied the checkerboard décor to the Ren Faire couture. Black and white chess kings crisscrossed right over the stranger's heart.

The man stared at me staring at him and smiled. "Fresh blood."

"Actually, Eric Deldridge." Eric strolled lazily into the room, seeming completely at ease chatting up the caped man. "While I am rather younger than most, I don't think the term *fresh blood* can rightfully be applied to me."

The cape man's smile broadened. "Eric Deldridge. I might have heard of you."

"Then it's even stranger that I have never had the pleasure of hearing of you." Eric reached the table and leaned in to shake hands with the cape man.

Some weird instinct made me move farther into the room. I don't know why. If cape man wanted to kill Eric, I don't know what I could have done about it. But I was Eric's apprentice, his second in the battle of life—at least, that's what I tried to tell myself.

"Kendrick McDonald." Cape man gave a little bow of his head. "And it should be a testament to this institution that you've never heard of The Game."

"What is The Game?" The words slipped from my mouth.

Kendrick glared at me as Eric shot me a warning look.

"The fresh blood speaks." Eric spread his arms wide, stepping aside for Kendrick McDonald.

"The Game is a place, and a thing. It's a way of life and death. It is meaning and power and you"—Kendrick leapt over the table, vaulting toward me—"you, fresh blood, might be an excellent new piece to play."

Kendrick stalked toward me, looking me up and down like I was a pretty girl and he was a gross construction worker.

"He's not a piece to play." Devon spoke so loudly his voice echoed around the room.

Kendrick leaned in, sniffing Devon. "You could play then. You won't survive, but it would be beautiful to watch you try."

"None of us want to play," Elizabeth said. "Whatever fancy game you think you've come up with, we're not interested."

"But you will be," Kendrick said. "Everyone loves The Game."

"If everyone wants to play, why did you need a Lancre to stalk my apprentice?" Eric's tone remained dry and conversational. Because, you know, I hadn't almost died or anything.

"Lancre," Kendrick said the word slowly. "Lancre?" he said again as though testing to be sure he really understood.

"You sent a Lancre to stalk a school." Eric paced the perimeter of the room, running his fingers along the backs of the leather booths and across the shining tabletops as though checking for dust. "The Lancre wasn't even very good, tried to take the girl instead of my apprentice. Your beast caused a fair bit of trouble as well. Made things unpleasant for us."

"*That* Lancre." Kendrick chuckled, nodding his understanding. "She's been out hunting for so long, I thought she'd been killed."

"You left a Lancre on the hunt with no supervision?" For the first time since entering The Game, anger sounded in Eric's voice.

"Don't be absurd!" Kendrick waved a hand in the air. "Could I supply The Game with fresh blood if I only had one, terribly unskilled Lancre hunting for me? We have some willing players, but they grow scarcer as the world begins to fear adventure. I have many Lancre."

"What?" Eric finally stopped pacing.

"I have Lancre in the city, across the country." Kendrick giggled. "I even have a few braving the far-flung reaches of Thailand, searching for something very special for me."

"You've set witch hunters free in the world!" Eric rounded on Kendrick. He seemed to grow in his rage as he walked slowly across the checkered floor. "You created monsters to kill our kind and told them to run along and have a good time?"

"Don't be absurd." A wide smile lit Kendrick's face. "If they killed their prey, who would there be to play The Game?"

Kendrick clapped his hands, and a *clang* shook the air. The door at the back of the room swung open, and a cage glided forward. The cage was partitioned into four quadrants, separated by thick metal bars, and each of the spaces held a thing in it.

"It's not too late for the fresh blood to join." Kendrick tilted his head, examining me once again. "He barely knows which end of a spell is pointy. Give me a month, and I'll have him fighting in The Game."

At the word *game* the things in the cage started to stir, coming to life like Kendrick had just set off their alarm clock.

"Bryant isn't going to play any game you have in mind." Devon stepped up to be shoulder to shoulder with me. He's voice was strong and sure, like he wasn't afraid of the cage that was still coming closer, or of the boy in the front of the cage who glared hatefully at me.

And it was a boy. A wild-looking boy near my age, dressed in black, furry leggings that were crusted in places, like he had forgotten to wash the blood of his enemies out of his clothes after a battle. In the front right corner there was a girl in a pure white, unstained dress. She didn't glare at me or even glance at Kendrick. She just stood with her back to us, moving her arms slowly through the air like she was doing some sort of demented warm-up.

There was a girl in black behind her, and a boy in white behind the other boy.

"These are the champions of the week," Kendrick cooed lovingly, like he was presenting his dog who had won best in show. "This one will earn out of the bars if he wins just once more this week." Kendrick trailed his fingers along the bars that trapped the boy in black.

"Is that what you do here?" Eric moved forward to examine the boy. "I had truly hoped it wouldn't be something so crude. I really must learn to lower my expectations."

"What are you talking about?" I asked. A prickle of understanding pressed on the back of my thoughts, but I couldn't get past the feral boy staring at me.

"Kendrick," Eric spat his name like it was a filthy word, "likes to kidnap young wizards and witches and train them to fight. Force them to fight. To the death would be my guess. It would have to be a very bloody sport to create enough income to support this expensive real estate."

"It is very lucrative." Kendrick rapped his knuckled against the cage. All four of the captives turned to stare at him. "And not just for me. It takes time to earn your way into the fights, time to earn your way out of indentures for the vast sums of money I put into my fighters' training, but if they can make it all the way through, they enter Manhattan free and stronger than anyone apprenticed to a coward who hides in the shadows of Beville could ever hope to be.

"So, what say you?" Kendrick pointed to me, and all the

heads in the cage swiveled toward me. "It's not too late for you to join me. And since you walked so nicely in, I won't add recruitment costs to your account. You'll be out of your indentures in no time."

"Recruitment?" Elizabeth growled. "I think you mean attempted murder and kidnapping."

"Spoken like a true mundane human," Kendrick sneered. "What are you going to do, little girl, call the police? They can't get up the stairs."

"Don't talk to her!" I shouted, feeling my feet carry me a step forward.

"And what will you do, fresh blood? Call the Ladies? Tell The Consortium to come after me?" Kendrick tossed his head back and roared with laughter. "Have you been cowering so deep in the shadows you haven't heard? The Ladies are in hiding, buried in the fortress of their Library. They won't risk leaving safety to come after the likes of me."

"What did you say?" Eric stepped forward, his hands tented under his chin in his usual thinking habit.

"There is no one left to police us!" Kendrick shouted, over-enunciating each word as though Eric were hard of hearing. "They are too weak to leave their Library without being destroyed. Holding onto the books is the only thing that keeps them in power. They will hide between the stacks until the end of time. They won't leave the Library. They can't stop me. You can't stop me. Nothing in the world can stop me!"

"I really must thank you." There was a cheerful note in Eric's tone that was more terrifying than furry-bloody-leggings dude clinging to the bars of his cage and baring his teeth at me. "I've spent two months trying to work out a problem, and you've just handed me the solution!" Eric let out a triumphant laugh. "Fate can be a cruel beast, but I am so grateful to her for bringing me here today!"

"You've apprenticed to a madman." Kendrick laughed. "And not even one who knows how to turn a profit."

"Life isn't about profit." Eric stepped forward, planting himself between us and Kendrick. "But I'm afraid I don't have time to work through your moral values or lack thereof. At your advice, I'm afraid our day has suddenly become quite busy."

"You really are a—"

"Of course"—Eric cut Kendrick off—"I can't leave you here to plot the kidnapping of anymore innocent young wizards either, and as you so kindly pointed out, law enforcement is rather lacking these days."

"Then we are at an impasse." Kendrick bowed, and the locks on the four cage doors *clicked*.

"Not at all," Eric said, ignoring the four fighters moving toward their now-open cage doors. "There are two ways forward. You can come with me, and I will bring you to a nice comfortable place where you will never be able to harm anyone again. Your fighters will be freed and sent to appropriate homes to be re-acclimated to magical society."

Furry leggings boy leapt silently to the floor.

"The second option is you refuse to come with me and I have to destroy your establishment, free your captives the hard way, and send the types of shadows after you that you will not escape."

The other fighters climbed out of their cages and stalked forward on the checkered floor.

"The types of shadows that track for me are unwilling to let their quarry survive," Eric continued like there weren't four creepy people closing in on him, not even bothering to spare them a glance. "This is an opportunity I won't offer again. Call off your dogs, or I'll have to call upon mine."

"You think you can fight me?" Kendrick asked so softly I

could barely hear him over the pounding of my pulse in my ears. "You think your little *dogs* can fight against my warriors."

"I find the term dog to be offensive," Devon said.

"I'd never call any of you a dog, Devon," Eric said. "And yes, we will fight you. And we will free the ones you have stolen from their homes."

A glimmer of joy shone in Kendrick's eyes. "Then let The Game begin!"

16

B right lights flicked on, shining down on the center of the room. If the booths had been filled with spectators, we might have been doing theatre in the round. But this wasn't going to end with everyone smiling and bowing.

Eric and Kendrick locked eyes with each other. With one fluid flip of the arms, Kendrick tossed off his fur cape.

"Elizabeth, take care of the door, please," Eric said calmly. "Bryant, try not to die."

"What the hell am I, chopped liver?" Devon asked.

The heads of the caged four turned toward Devon.

"More like bait, but I thought it rude to say. *Kunga!*" Eric slipped the spell in at the end of his sentence. Kendrick doubled over and flew backward as though something very strong had kicked him hard in the stomach.

Then it started all at once.

The two dressed in white launched themselves at Devon.

"*Primurgo!*" I shouted. I didn't have time to make sure the shield was enough to protect Devon. The two in black had charged straight toward me.

The girl screamed something at such a manic pitch I

couldn't hear the word, but white-hot pain cut deep into my shoulder.

"*Milkawa!*" I focused on the black square under the girl's feet. The floor writhed and squirmed, slithering silently around her ankles.

The boy with the fur pants didn't shout a spell at me. He just leapt into the air, arms outstretched like he wanted to give me a lethal bear hug.

"*Primurgo!*" I shouted an instant too late. With a horrible *smack*, the boy crashed into me, knocking me to the ground. Stars danced in front of my eyes so brightly I almost didn't see him pull his fist back. "*Abalata!*" A thick blackness sprouted from my hand, and I threw it at the boy's face, knocking him sideways off of me.

The girl in black screamed in rage. Blue light jetted from her palm, and I rolled away, yelping as the spell blazed past, burning my ear.

"*Erunca!*" I knew what the spell was going to do, but seeing the lightning shoot from the ceiling and strike the girl made me gag. But I didn't have time to consider the morality of unleashing lightning on someone who had been locked in a cage for who knows how long. Devon was screaming.

I turned toward him, sure I was going to see my best friend die. But Devon was still standing and very much alive, holding a chunk of table in his hands and swinging it at the girl in white, who had blood trickling down her cheek.

"Bryant, door!" Devon shouted.

I spun to Elizabeth, who ran her fingers along the crack of the closed metal door.

"Bryant, floor door!" A sharp, black something flew at Devon and landed in his table chunk with a *thud*. "Now, Bry!"

I don't know if it was a lifetime of friendship or sudden brilliance, but I knew exactly what Devon wanted me to do.

Focusing as hard as I could on the floor at the girl's feet, I shouted, "*Portunda!*" The floor split perfectly along the lines of the checkerboard, creating a two-square by four-square hole right beneath her feet. The girl fell with a shriek.

"*Portundo!*" The hole in the floor sealed back up with *crack*.

"Bryant, duck!" Devon shouted as a painful weight crashed into my back, sending me face first onto the floor.

I coughed, trying to pull enough air into my lungs to speak as something hard pushed into the back of my neck.

With a shout of pain, the weight disappeared. I rolled over in time to see fur pants hit the ceiling. Eric had turned away from his own fight with Kendrick to help me.

Kendrick had both hands in the air, rearing back as though preparing for a deathblow.

"*Stasio!*" I spat the word and leapt to my feet. The spell wouldn't hold Kendrick for long, but Devon was under a table and the boy in white loomed over him, his fingers crackling with a spell.

"*Turso!*" A band of white lashed out at the boy's ankles, knocking him off his feet.

"Let's go!" Elizabeth shouted from the open door.

I didn't have time to wonder how Elizabeth had opened the door without magic. I darted to the table and hauled Devon to his feet.

"You can't run from The Game!" Kendrick shouted.

"Looks like we can!" Devon called back as we tore through the door and onto the stairs. Eric was out a moment behind us, muttering some long spell I didn't try to understand as we bolted for the next level.

The sounds coming from below were so blissfully normal. Awkwardly exciting music and the dull chatter of tourists. For a split second I thought we were just going to keep running. Down to the street and to someplace quiet where Eric could heal my shoulder and Devon's head. We rounded the corner and were nearly to the next flight of stairs when streaks of bright blue shot through the doorway. I tackled Elizabeth, pinning her out of reach of the spell.

My heart thudded out of control. I waited to hear screams of terror from the innocent diners, but all that came was a roar of tumultuous applause.

I jumped up, blocking Elizabeth from the doorway. At the far end of the room stood the girl dressed in white, purple flames crackling around her fingertips.

"The Game won't let you go." The girl's voice carried perfectly over the crowd.

It wasn't the pronouncement of doom that made my stomach drop to my toes. It was her voice. It was so...normal. Like any girl I would have talked to at school, if talking to girls were a thing I ever really did. She didn't sound demonically evil or even psychotic. She was just a girl who had been captured and brought here. Made to live in a cage and fight.

I was one magic cellphone and a crazy guy in a black suit away from being her.

"You don't have to do this!" I stepped forward, reaching my hands out toward her. "You don't have to fight for Kendrick. You can come with us."

The girl stared at me, tilting her head to the side. She didn't move as I cut through the tables, weaving my way toward her. "Just come with us, and you'll be safe."

"I've never seen them do this scene before," a woman's nasal voice cut over my words, breaking whatever truce the girl and I had.

"There is no life without winning The Game." Purple flames flew from the girl's hand, streaming toward me.

"*Aarantha!*" I caught the fire in the twister that formed around me. Clawing my hands through the air, I pulled the vortex into my palm, aiming it up toward the ceiling above, keeping the flames away from the bystanders.

People clapped and cheered as the vibrantly purple flames licked the ceiling.

Two men with glowing swords stepped forward.

"The Game will not be disturbed," one of the men said, raising his saber. It was sort of comical—him standing there in his pajama-like, white costume, glaring at me.

"I don't care about your game." Sweat dripped down my face from the sheer effort of keeping the flames away from the spectators.

"You haven't won your round yet." A woman in a red-and-black costume stepped forward, pointing her laser gun at my chest.

"I really think I'm starting to understand why you thought this fandom blending was so annoying, Bry. Ensigns and light sabers don't mesh well." Devon stepped up to stand next to me. "We're leaving, so back the hell off."

"You can't leave without winning." The girl in white let go of the fire spell, and the violet flames dissipated.

Like they had plotted it in the break room, the two space ninjas charged forward, light sabers raised.

A laugh rose in my throat before turning into a stone of fear as the glowing swords got closer to us. They weren't fake plastic glowing tubes or even the nicer Comic-Con variety. The blades of the swords crackled with very real, very dangerous magic as they slashed toward Devon and me.

"*Primurgo!*" I shouted. The blades of the sabers sparked as they struck my shield.

The woman dressed in red-and-black military attire started shooting at us with her laser gun. The globules of magic shook my shield, and the crowd roared.

"Drop the shield, Bry!" Devon shouted.

I let go of the shield as a chair flew over my shoulder, hitting one of the space ninjas in the stomach. Devon bull charged forward and, for a split second, I was absolutely positive I was going to see my best friend split right down the middle.

"*Abalata!*" I threw the black taffy from my hand, hitting the other sword bearer in the face.

Eric was on top of the tables, leaping from one to the next, dodging the blazing spells being shot by the space army chick. There was something building in his hands—a ball of crackling green light. He threw it at the woman, tossing her into a table, which crumpled to the ground. The crowd's cheering turned instantly to shouts of anger and fear.

"This way!" Elizabeth called from the far wall.

I glanced to Devon, who was on his feet, holding a sparking red sword. The man he had taken it from lay unconscious on the ground behind him.

"You can't leave The Game!" the girl in white roared as we ran for the far wall.

"*Parapus!*" Eric shouted.

Thin black lines flew through the air, binding the girl.

"*Kunga!*"

The girl doubled over as the air was knocked from her.

Elizabeth stood next to a plain, gray wall with shimmering panels on the floor. A console of buttons stood to one side.

"Hold on!" Elizabeth called as Eric leapt onto the glowing platform.

A shimmering swirl of glittery strobe lights clouded my vision as the floor disappeared from under my feet.

17

Before I had time to scream we had passed through a chunk of black and were falling onto a squishy floor. Metal netting and thick bars obscured our view of the room outside. But the crowd in the steam punk dining room seemed to be totally calm as a monster walked through the rows of tables, holding a tray of display deserts.

"I almost fell on my sword," Devon panted, pushing himself to his feet, clasping a silver cylinder in his hand. "I almost killed myself with my light saber." With a flick of his wrist, the red blade sprouted from the silver tube, blossoming to magical life complete with a low hum. "Thank God they went for geek accuracy."

"We need to go. Now." I reached for the glow-taped knob on the elevator door.

The door was much lighter than it looked, like the metal netting was really only plastic in disguise. It swung open easily, and a spotlight flicked on, beaming right on the fake elevator. Every head in the dining room swiveled toward us.

My mouth went Sahara dry, and my hands started to shake

in a way they hadn't when people were trying to kill me only a moment before.

"Come on." Elizabeth slid her hand into mine and dragged me out of the elevator and onto the little stage in front of it.

"They're not even supposed to be on this floor!" a prepubescent twerp shouted from his seat right in front of the stage. "They aren't monsters."

"You have no idea what monsters are, little boy," Eric said, taking his place at the front of our pack. "I assure you if you knew what really lurked in the shadows, you would never sleep again."

All the color drained from the boy's face and his lips trembled.

"The quality of service here is terrible," the boy's mother snapped.

"You have no idea, lady." Devon raised his sword as the door to the hall filled with mismatched employees.

The boy in furry black leggings stood at the center, flanked by space people, Frankenstein's monster, and a mad scientist.

"We are going to leave this building." Eric's voice echoed around the room like he was wearing a body mic. "You can either step aside and let us leave peacefully, or you can make us fight you."

The kitchen door swung open, and a line of bussers filed in, holding their trays up like shields.

"Not human, not human, not human," Elizabeth murmured in a panicked voice.

I tried to see what she was seeing beyond the uniforms and angry faces.

"Fine, we'll fight our way out." Eric raised both his hands. "But I absolutely refuse to apologize for any structural damage. *Elihi nustrum alief*"—Eric began walking toward the door, pushing with every step like he was trying to move a city bus by himself—"*manheil erbracina!*"

For one terrible moment, I thought the spell had gone horribly wrong and wasn't going to do anything but leave Eric closer to the flock of people who wanted to kill us.

But then a bright light flashed between Eric's hands, exploding out into a wall of light that shook the air and blasted the group off their feet. Frankenstein's monster's mask flew off his face as he smacked into the banister. Through the bright wall Eric had created I could tell something wasn't quite right. The monster's features were too animalistic, his nose too small, his mouth too large. For one moment of stupidity, I wanted to ask Elizabeth if she saw what I was seeing and if that was what the world looked like to her all the time. But Eric had started to sag under his spell.

"We have to get out of here." Devon charged forward, wrapping his left arm around Eric's waist while holding his sword in his right hand.

The line of busboys charged toward them, bellowing madly.

"*Erunca!*" I shouted, and lighting streaked from the chipped paint on the ceiling.

Only one of the busboys was quick enough to raise his shield and block my spell. The lightning bounced off the metal and hit the ceiling, leaving a black scorch mark where it struck.

The man lunged toward Eric and Devon, giving no sign he had noticed my attack at all.

"Devon, watch out!" As the words tore from my throat, Devon swung his sword, slicing through the busboy's wrist.

Everything in the world slowed as the busboy's gloved hand flew through the air, tumbling wrist over fingers until it landed with a *smack* right in the center of a table full of teenage girls.

"Move, move, move!" Elizabeth shouted over the shrieks of the girls.

Eric's spell faded from view as we ran toward the door. The ones who had been trying to block our path were sprawled on the floor. Large dents cracked the wall where bodies had struck plaster.

"Bryant, above us," Eric said, his voice weaker than I had ever heard, lacking its usual suave flare.

I glanced up as the *rumble* of footsteps pounded down the stairs.

"*Limbargo!*" I shouted at the banister, which grew into a cage-like barrier as we ran down the steps to the ground floor.

"*Expulso!*" a high voice shouted from the bottom of the stairs. A thick stream of red shot up the steps. I slammed myself into the wall just in time, pinning Elizabeth behind me.

"*Kunga*," Eric rasped, knocking away the attacker.

But orders were being shouted in a horribly familiar voice. "Do not let them leave!"

At the bottom of the steps, the street came into view through the glass of the door. Masses still packed the street outside, desperate to come enjoy the kitsch, completely unaware people were trying to murder us.

Two men holding wands charged out of the bar, their long black robes billowing around them like they were filming a bad music video. One of the men flourished his wand.

"*Abalata!*" I screamed, terrified of what the wand might do. The black that flew from my palm knocked both the men's wands out of their hands.

"Good one, Bry!" Devon shouted, grabbing the handle to the outside door and moving to wrench it open. But the doorframe shifted and melted as Kendrick stepped calmly out of the bar, clapping his hands.

"You've done well." Kendrick smiled, like it was merely impressive that we had destroyed most of his restaurant and potentially killed a few of his people in the process of fighting for our lives. "Better than I thought. Making it all the way to the ground floor. Even the pretty, normal boy managed to find a way to make himself useful."

"Thanks," Devon growled.

Footfalls thumped on the steps as steampunk monsters, space soldiers, and intergalactic ninjas penned us in from above.

"I really think at this point you should be able to appreciate what we're accomplishing here." Kendrick spread his arms wide as a line of wand-bearing wizards formed behind him. "Look at the order I've created, the power. Isn't it worth a little bit of death and pain to be a part of something so wonderful?"

"There are very few things I believe are worth dying for." Eric pulled himself to stand up straight. "Forcing innocent children to fight will never be one of them."

"Well if they won't join you..." Kendrick shrugged. "Kill them."

A dozen wands raised toward us, glowing swords hummed to life above us, and for the tenth time since I met Eric Deldridge, I thought, *This is how I die.*

"The real pity is you didn't even get the wizards right," Eric said. "Real wizards don't need wands."

"*Dothranta!*" I shouted the spell as I leapt toward the door. Before I reached the solid wall, everything around me went black. I felt Devon moving next to me, raising his saber. "Don't kill me!" I yipped, before shouting. "*Portunda!* Elizabeth!" I called her name as the edge of the door reformed under my fingertips.

"*Tundina!*" Eric shouted the spell, and a horrible *whirr* sounded as I dragged Elizabeth and Devon out the door.

"Eric!" I bellowed as bright sunlight blinded me. "Eric!"

Elizabeth's hand slipped from mine as she dove for the door.

"Elizabeth, no!" I screamed, moving to charge after her, terrified the darkness I had created would swallow her forever.

Devon grabbed me around the middle, holding me back.

"Elizabeth!" Her name tore at my throat. "Elizabeth!"

Before I could break out of Devon's grasp, Elizabeth reappeared, her arm around Eric as he stumbled next to her.

"Block the door," Elizabeth ordered.

"*Portundo.*" The spell fell from my lips, making the door meld in with the rest of the restaurant front.

The crowd on the sidewalk clapped and shouted their approval of our show.

"Let's get out of here." Devon flicked off his sword and took Elizabeth's place, supporting Eric.

"We have to mark it," Eric mumbled, his face scary pale. Redness surrounded his eyes. "*Envasio.*"

A shimmering black X four stories tall appeared on the front of the building. It wasn't flat like paint. It shimmered and swirled like it had mass of its own. A hypnotizing mark with no non-magical explanation.

"The Ladies won't be able to ignore that." Eric smiled and sagged into Devon's arms.

Elizabeth led us through the gawking crowd and around the corner. My heart pounded like we were running for our lives. I mean, we had just left a horde of people/maybe-not-so-much-people that wanted to kill us. But Elizabeth walked calmly, and I don't think Eric could have run anyway.

It wasn't until we were two blocks away that any of us even spoke.

"Where do we want to go?" Elizabeth asked when we reached a set of steps leading down to the subway. There were a dozen entrances to Beville scattered around the city, all of them I knew of branching from the subway system.

"We should go to Beville, get Eric some help," I began, but Eric spoke over me.

"We need to get to the Statue of Liberty." Eric's voice rasped as he spoke. "We need to get to the ferry."

"Not until you've rested," Devon said. "You look like you're going to die any second. Let's go to Lola's, have her patch you up."

"We've just given the Ladies a reason to leave the Library." Eric wobbled toward the subway steps. "We might not have another opportunity like this for a very long time. Besides, a little rest and I'll be right as rain."

"I don't think—" I argued, but Elizabeth cut me off this time.

"He's right. We need to go now." She threaded her fingers through mine. "We have to keep going."

There was something in the definitive way she spoke that kept Devon and me from arguing as we hopped the train toward Battery Park.

We were too far south for the tourists to crush us on the subway. The rumble of the tracks under our feet soothed the adrenaline that made me want to kick through the door and run into the dark screaming for help. I guess if you spend your whole life in New York City, the swaying of the subway trains is practically like being rocked to sleep.

"Could you see in the dark?" Eric asked Elizabeth, his head leaning back against the subway window in a most un-Eric like way.

"What?" Elizabeth asked, sliding into the seat beside him. I hadn't even realized he was the only one to sit until she joined him.

"You came into the darkness of Bryant's spell to find me," Eric explained. "I need to know if you could see in the spell. If the spell is vulnerable to seers, we can't use it anymore."

"I couldn't see." Elizabeth sighed. "I just knew about where you were and like you enough to risk going back for you."

"Then I am both relieved and honored." Eric gave a tiny bow

of the head that looked like he might have been falling asleep, but the train rumbled to a stop and it was time to walk again.

That's the weirdest thing about fighting. When you leave it seems like everything in the whole world should be in chaos. Like every person you pass should look terrified after the things you've seen.

But that's not how it works, at least not when you're fighting secretive magical battles. No one is supposed to know about things that can kill you with a spell, so they don't know to be afraid. They keep moving through their lives blissfully unaware, leaving you to stagger through their midst. Trying not to look like demons might be chasing you.

18

No one attacked us on our way to Battery Park. I held my breath as I passed over my black emergency credit card to pay for our tickets. I had destroyed part of my school (again) and run away from home. There was a very large possibility my dad had finally decided to cut me off and the card was now nothing more than a magnetized bookmark. But the card went through, and the lady handed us our tickets without even looking up from her computer. I magicked away the dirt and rubble from our clothes so the security guard didn't even give us a second glance as we climbed aboard the ferry.

The wind on the water was even more biting than it had been on land. Like it was determined to freeze off layers of our skin and rip them away forever. Part of me wanted it to.

"We should sit inside." Elizabeth glanced meaningfully at Eric.

He was just as pale as he'd been on the train, his eyes half closed as he gripped the rail to keep standing.

"Good idea." My voice came out all stupid and high like it always did when I was trying to sound calm and cool. "I'll grab us some cocoa."

"I prefer tea, personally," Eric said.

"Me, too." Devon took Eric's elbow, escorting him into the overheated interior of the boat.

There weren't many people inside. It was too late in the day for most people to be heading out for the Statue of Liberty and Ellis Island experience. Rows of upholstered, uncomfortable seats faced a giant TV playing a history film. In the back corner there were a few sticky looking tables. Devon led Eric that way.

"Do you think he'll be all right?" Elizabeth whispered to me as we waited at the snack counter.

"Aren't you the one who agreed we couldn't take him to be healed?" I muttered before turning to the girl at the counter. "Two cocoas, two hot teas, and four sandwiches." I hadn't realized how horribly hungry I was until I said the word *sandwiches*. We had spent the morning battling in a restaurant, but we hadn't actually gotten around to eating anything.

"What kind of sandwiches?" The girl pointed grumpily at the menu. "There are choices you have to make."

Choices. Like running for the Statue of Liberty instead of taking Eric somewhere to rest. Choices like attacking kids who had been locked in cages for who knows how long.

"Well?" the girl asked with an overly-dramatic eye roll.

"Four turkey sandwiches on wheat, and chips with all of them," Elizabeth answered for me.

I squeezed her hand, grateful she hadn't made me think about what we all should eat. I didn't even know how we had managed to stay alive.

I didn't really feel like I knew anything at all. We had gone to find out who was after me and had come out of the restaurant from Hell with way more questions than we'd woken up with that morning. I'd lightninged someone, Devon had chopped off a dude's hand, and Eric looked like he might die any minute. The only one who seemed to have it together was Elizabeth.

Elizabeth, who I was supposed to protect. Who I didn't know how to protect. And now we were on a ferry where our escape route would involve swimming in freezing cold, contaminated water.

Anger rumbled in my empty stomach. I didn't even know why we were on a boat, let alone why we were doing the New York tourist day planned by Satan.

"You okay?" Elizabeth asked in a hushed tone as the food girl collected our purchases at sloth speed.

"No." The word weighed heavily in my mouth. "I'm an idiot who felt like I was actually starting to get a handle on all this. But now I feel like I'm drowning again."

Elizabeth leaned in, brushing her lips gently against mine. All the anger and fear and panic melted away in her soft flowery scent. After an all too brief moment, she pulled away and looked into my poop-brown eyes with her perfect sparkly ones.

"You do have a handle on it. You used magic today like I've never seen you use it before. The four of us fought together, and we all walked out alive and really pretty unharmed." She took both my hands in hers. "There's a lot of things I don't understand either, but we'll make Eric explain. And what he doesn't know, we'll all figure out together. We're going to be okay, Bryant."

"Is that the gorgeous girlfriend or the beautiful seer talking?" I asked, quasi-hoping she would say she had seen a prophecy in sewer trash that meant this was all going to work out okay.

"Just your girlfriend." Elizabeth smiled, and my heart did a back handspring at the word *girlfriend*. "Who believes in her boyfriend and in her friends. We'll make it out of this."

A freezing gust of wind blew open the backdoor, sending flyers flying and the crewmembers sprinting to slam it shut. The wind stopped as soon as the door was rammed closed, but the cold feeling on my neck didn't go away.

"Do you want your food or not?" the counter girl said snidely.

We grabbed our overpriced meal and headed back to our table in the corner.

Eric sat slumped on one side with Devon across from him. Eric's eyes were closed, but he was speaking as Elizabeth slid into the booth next to him.

"There is no healing that I require," Eric murmured.

"Then what's wrong with you?" I asked, pulling my turkey sandwich from its cellophane wrapping.

"I used a spell too strong for my weak, mortal frame." Eric opened his eyes to stare right at me. "A thing which I highly suggest you never try. I barely survived the damnable thing. I doubt my charming apprentice would fare much better."

"If you knew the spell was too much for you, why did you use it?" Devon leaned across the table. "Or did you just try a spell without knowing what it would do?"

"Devon," Elizabeth whispered warningly.

"I think it's a legitimate question." Devon snatched a sandwich. "Is our fearless leader stupid or suicidal?"

"I would never try a spell without a relatively good idea of the consequences, unlike some people." Eric gave me serious side-eye as he took a long drink of tea, grimacing at the paper cup. "We were in a desperate situation that called for an unusual amount of magic to ensure our survival."

"And what if we hadn't been there to haul you out of the devil's meat shop?" Devon ripped the cellophane off his sandwich so violently you'd think it was the bread that had tried to kill us. "Would you just have asked for a time out so you could sit down for a little nap?"

"I wouldn't have used magic that strong if I didn't have people I trusted fighting by my side," Eric said. "If I thought for one moment any of you might leave me lying defenseless on the floor, I would have used normal amounts of magic to find an escape route for one. But as I trust you not to abandon me, it seemed prudent to find a way for all of us to escape."

Eric and Devon silently glared at each other while I took a few bites of my dry turkey sandwich.

"If we've established no one has a death wish and we all actually do like each other in some twisted way, would someone please explain to me why we're going to the Statue of Liberty? Not that I'm opposed to a historical field trip, but I thought we were going to try and stop the Ladies from killing all of us." Elizabeth took a sip of her cocoa.

"We're going to the Library," Eric answered.

"But the Library is up by Central Park. The entrance is at The Consortium, we've seen it," I said, wondering if Eric's use of too much magic had somehow affected his brain.

I knew I was right. We had seen at least the outside of The Consortium while we were hunting for Eric back in the days when he was still trying to kill us. The place looked like a normal, if unpopular, café on Central Park West from the outside, but the Ladies ran the place. It was the only outpost of magic aboveground in Manhattan. I guess the only *official* outpost would be more accurate. We had just blasted our way through a magical dining experience, after all.

"The primary entrance to the Library is, in fact, under The Consortium." Eric leaned his head against the wall. "But the Library isn't one basement of books. It's a vast system of tunnels holding the entire knowledge of magical civilization. It is a vast *living* space."

"I'm sorry, you emphasized the word *living*?" My throat was suddenly too dry to take another bite of gross sandwich. I tried to gulp my hot chocolate and burned my throat instead.

"Magic imbues the things it touches with magic," Eric said, slipping into his terse, teaching tone. "It changes places and things. My home isn't just a building—it has a spirit all its own. Beville isn't just a cave—it is a living, breathing place. You may not be astute enough to have noticed, but if you survive to return, taste the air in Beville. It's not the dank stench of a cave. The air is crisp and sweet with magic. Now take that magic, all that magic, and condense it into its truest form, into knowledge itself. Vast stores of knowledge. The most potent and pure form of magic available. Lock it away for centuries and see how the walls change, how they breathe, how they move. I've heard tales of the Library rearranging the volumes all on its own. Organizing the world to its will. Presenting the magic it wants to be used."

"Wow," I breathed.

"Have you seen it?" Elizabeth asked, her eyes wide with wonder. "Do the books fly around? Or just transport instantly?"

"I have no idea." Eric sat up straight, his eyes looking more alert by the minute. "Other than the Ladies, no living person has been in the Library."

"Again with the *living*," I sighed.

"Thaden." Devon leaned across the table. "Thaden got in, didn't he?"

"Indeed he did," Eric began. "Thaden might have been evil—"

"Most definitely evil," I tossed in.

"But he was a genius, a very magically powerful genius. Many had tried to break into the Library before, but none had ever succeeded." Eric tore open five sugar packets and began dumping them out onto the table one by one. "Most died in the attempt. Years of theories and rumors led Thaden into the Library. Once I heard someone had managed to see the vast stores of our kind's most precious treasure, I knew I had to try it for myself."

"Of course you did." Devon shook his head.

Eric didn't seem to notice. He patted the pile of sugar on the table flat and picked up a stir stick. "I followed the same rumors that led Thaden on his successful quest. I found a way into the Library. And I was close, so wonderfully close, to breaking through. I failed." Eric traced lines in the sugar with the stick. "But I escaped with my life. A feat great enough to attract Thaden's attention. He had created the phone by then, using the magic he had taken from the Library. He told me of its glory, everything I sought deep underground handed to me in one convenient package. So I abandoned my dreams of entering the Library and joined Thaden's service."

"We all know how well that went," I said.

"Terribly well by all accounts." Eric didn't look up from his drawing. "We're all alive and stronger for having each other."

"It would almost sound sweet if I thought there weren't some near-death about to be added to that sentiment," Elizabeth said.

"And now we're going to have to succeed where I alone failed." Eric finally looked up, a hint of a smile twinkling in his eyes. "Kendrick was right. We don't need to search for each of the Ladies and fight them on the streets. That could take years. They would recruit new members to carry on their grudge against poor Bryant."

"And you, don't you dare leave out you," I interrupted, pointing an angry finger at him, which he ignored.

"The new members would hunt us as viciously as the Ladies we have already encountered. To gain our freedom we have to destroy the pillar on which they stand, the thing that gives them power over wizards. We have to take the Library. Without it, the Ladies cannot rule. They cannot attack us."

"You want to destroy the Library?" Devon said loudly enough that the few people trying to watch the Statue of Liberty film turned to glare at him.

"I would never dream of harming the Library in any way,"

Eric said. "I would rather die than risk damaging such a treasure. What I am suggesting is evicting the Ladies."

"You want to break into the Library and kick the Ladies out?" Devon whisper-shouted.

"Basically." Eric shrugged and set down the stir stick. "And lucky for you, I'm one of the few people who has attempted to break into the Library and survived."

"Now I feel great about it," Devon said.

"And I have a team with me this time." Eric leaned forward. "I know the where, and now I have the tools."

"Now we're tools," Devon growled.

"That still doesn't explain why we're on a boat heading toward the great metal lady." Elizabeth pointed out the window.

The statue had come into view through the glass, as green-tinted and surreal as ever, towering above the water. If this had been a normal school field trip, it would have been cool. I'd have taken a picture of the beacon of hope that greeted immigrants and felt grateful for living in a country where a lady with a torch could mean so much to so many.

Staring at her with overly sweet cocoa in my mouth, she looked like a sentry standing guard, blocking my hopes and dreams for survival with her giant green book of doom.

Eric tapped the table next to his flattened sugar pile. I had thought it was a nervous tick, his way of dealing with feeling like a steaming pile of poop, but he hadn't been doodling—he'd been drawing a map.

A long curve marked the west side of Manhattan with a *C* marking The Consortium's location on Central Park West. There was a long thin shape marked *BV* under the Village right over Beville. And crossing under the city, out into the water, and toward a crudely-drawn Statue of Liberty was a swatch marked with an *L*.

"The entrance to the Library that is officially listed is under

The Consortium. But the Library expands well outside the city, down below the water where very special sorts of magic dwell. After all, if you're going to go through the trouble of digging, you may as well dig for something good."

"They mined for magic?" Elizabeth asked.

"Exactly." Eric nodded. "And it all might have come to nothing. I have no idea if the Ladies ever found anything under the earth they so diligently mined. But the work proved useful when the time came to build a second entrance to the Library. The world went to war, and it began to seem possible New York City could be attacked, even taken by foreign powers. That is when the Ladies built an escape route, lengthening the Library to give themselves a cozy place aboveground they could run to if foreign wizards stormed their gates."

"They would abandon the Library?" Devon asked. "That might make this easier."

"They would destroy it," Eric corrected. "Better to let the knowledge of the ages burn than have it in someone else's hands."

"But we're going to try and take it?" I squeaked. "What if they set the Library to self-destruct?"

"Then we burn with the books, but"—Eric held up a hand as I tried to speak again—"they won't do it while they're inside. And if the legends are as reliable as I am hoping, they would need to be at the statue exit to make it work at all."

"So if legends are right, and we can do something only an evil mastermind has managed, and if nothing goes wrong, *then* we'll drive the Ladies from the Library and take charge of magic in Manhattan?" Devon leaned back, crossing his arms over his chest.

"More than just Manhattan," I said. "The world. It's the Library for the whole world."

19

One thing I've learned about planning world domination or at least deadly attacks—it makes your stomach feel like it's made of cement. Like the weight of the world you're now trying to take charge of was in the awful turkey sandwich you bought on the ferry ride to your doom.

"It isn't the only library of magic in the whole world." Eric waved a breezy hand through the air like what he was talking about wasn't monumental and quite possibly disastrous. "Just the largest and most notable. Honestly, I have more books hidden in my home than the London Library has on its shelves."

"So best, most important library in the world, run by the murdering Ladies who are in charge of basically everything." I swallowed hard. It was good to know I could still swallow while panicking. "Just some sensible world domination for our afternoon enjoyment."

"We aren't plotting world domination, Bryant." Elizabeth reached across the table and took my hand. "We're going in to kick out some bad people."

Her soft, delicate hand in mine made the stomach cement melt away.

"And once we get rid of the bad people?" Devon asked, his brows knit together.

"We'll figure that part out if we survive," Eric said as a voice came over the speakers.

"*We are now arriving at the Statue of Liberty. Please check under your seats for your belongings, and keep your groups together. The last ferry leaves at 6 p.m. this evening. Please arrive at the docks no later than 5:50 for boarding.*"

The buzz of people moving toward the doors blocked out the rest of the words.

"Anything of interest, Elizabeth?" Eric asked as the herd moved us out the doors and into the freezing air on the deck.

"That kid stuck gum under the railing." Elizabeth pointed to a snot-nosed ginger in front of us.

"Splendid." Eric led the way onto the dock that ran up to the tiny island.

I had been to visit Lady Liberty for school field trips. Like six times. I had always taken the wide path straight to the front of the island where you could take a picture of the statue. Most of the people who got off the ferry shambled along that same route.

"Please don't tell me we have to climb to the top and jump off," I whispered, trying to sound like I was joking even though I was afraid that might be exactly what we needed to do.

"Don't be ridiculous." Eric shook his head, tipping his face up to the winter sun as we followed the flock of tourists. "We're going to find a quiet place to hide ourselves until the island has cleared and we can slip away."

"Until the island has cleared?" Devon said. "Why didn't we just bring your boat over here once the statue closed for the day?"

Devon had a point. Eric did have a little sailboat we'd ridden on while fleeing from the Ladies the first time we were all facing imminent death.

"Do you have any idea how much security there is around this island?" Eric asked, standing in the center of the path, casually scanning every person that passed. "Better to sneak out than in."

"And where do we wait?" Elizabeth asked. "And please tell me it'll be warm."

"Right..." Eric paused for a long moment, beckoning us all to the very edge of the path, before sweeping a hand through the air. "Here."

I noticed the change in noise first. It was like someone had clapped earmuffs onto my head.

"What?" Devon asked, his voice sounding perfectly normal, but as the nasty little gum boy passed, I could see his mouth moving as he shouted at his mother, but there was no real sound.

"Cool," I breathed.

"Now if we could all take a few more steps into the trees," Eric said in a tour guide voice.

"Don't tell me the spell moves with us." Giddiness bubbled inside me. "Okay, tell me the spell moves with us."

"It can shift slightly," Eric said in an exasperated tone. "Enough to get us off the path."

"And they can't see us?" Elizabeth traced her fingers through the air, which shimmered as flesh met spell.

"Or hear us. And just for you, Miss Wick." Eric gave a little bow. "*Relanto.*" The air around us warmed at once.

"You can wave your hand and make an impenetrable shield?" Devon growled. He alone didn't seem to be happy about the instant comfort.

"There is more to it than waving your hand. *Glasien.*" At Eric's word, the ground in the tent/shield glowed faintly for a moment. The chill disappeared from under my feet as the snow vanished, replaced by squishy, fresh grass.

"Nice," Elizabeth sighed and sank to the ground.

"Do you know how many times survival would have been significantly less painful if you had just waved your hand and made a shield?" Devon spat. "I can count two today."

Eric sighed, holding up both hands placatingly as Devon took a breath to keep railing.

"This sort of shield isn't useful in combat," Eric began. "It's too passive. A spell meant to harm could fly right through it. All it does is make a nice little silencing bubble with a touch of camouflage and a few dashes of something fancy that dissuades people from trying to walk through it. It does no good if someone is looking for you or if you are in an enclosed space. But for now it will give us all a chance to gain some much needed rest."

Devon stared at Eric, stone-faced. He looked like a racially ambiguous, clothed version of the David. Handsome, unflinching marble.

"Fine," Devon said after a very tense minute. "Just fine." He lay down on the newly formed grass, coat and all, his eyes fixed on the bare tree branches above us.

I wanted to talk to him, to ask him why he was so mad at Eric for being normal douche Eric, but we were trapped in an invisible tent with tourists unknowingly passing a few feet from Devon's head, so it didn't seem like the time.

"Do you see anything of interest, Elizabeth?" Eric asked again.

Elizabeth silently scanned the trees and people moving past. "Nothing magical."

"Good." Eric smiled tiredly and pulled off his jacket. With a perfect flick of the wrist, he laid it out on the ground and sat on the silk lining.

"Right." I pulled off my long coat. I didn't bother with the wrist flicking to lay it out flat. I just knelt and spread it out like a mere human. Then I held out my hand. Elizabeth took it and scooted over to sit on my coat. And suddenly I wasn't a stupid human lacking magical sophistication. I was a brave knight giving a beautiful lady a soft place to rest.

"What did you see in the restaurant?" Devon asked.

"Things." Elizabeth gave a little shudder. "People that weren't quite people. Their faces were wrong, or maybe darkness had taken bits of them."

"And Kendrick had them working in a restaurant?" I tried not to picture a server with a black void instead of an arm bringing me dinner.

"Kendrick is much cleverer than I had hoped, clever enough that I doubt we've seen the last of him. I expect he will be long gone by the time the Ladies reach The Game. "

"Great," I muttered.

"But if he's so smart, why did he put not quite people right in view of the tourists?" Elizabeth asked.

"He didn't. He dressed them up as characters or hid them in unnoticeable positions."

"The costume part I sort of understand. If I couldn't *see*, I probably wouldn't have noticed," Elizabeth said. "But it was super noticeable when the bussers attacked."

"When they were forced to defend The Game, then yes, it became noticeable," Eric explained. "But on any normal day, no one would notice anything strange because they refuse to look. You've asked before why Lola's associates appear to be homeless?"

"Yeah," I answered.

"The same reason bussers are an excellent disguise for the not quite humans or wizards in Kendrick's employ. Both are the type no one really wants to look at. No one wants to look the homeless man or the underpaid in the face. They don't want to acknowledge that part of the reality in which they so comfortably live. If you don't want to see something at all, imagine how hard it would be to see something awful in it."

"Unless, of course, you're a seer." Elizabeth sighed and curled up on my coat. "Then you get to see everything in every dark shadow and corner."

Eric gave a nod. "A terrible burden that is a great gift to our cause."

"Well, the gift is exhausting." Elizabeth yawned. "Wake me up if someone tries to kill us."

Her streaked hair splayed out around her like something in an art museum. Then she did the most amazing thing. Without even opening her eyes she reached up and took my hand, gently pulling me down to lie behind her. She wrapped my arm over her like a blanket and sighed, like because I had become her big spoon she felt safe.

Everything inside me melted, and I didn't care about the death-defying mission we were on. I was holding Elizabeth. My heart buzzed, and I held her tighter, letting my face touch the back of her hair, breathing in her delicious scent.

I closed my eyes, not caring if Devon and Eric thought I looked like an idiot. My arm rose and fell with each breath Elizabeth took. Soon her breathing was so slow and steady. I knew she was asleep. And I spun into blissful oblivion.

———

"You couldn't think I would forget it."

Eric's voice pulled me from sleep. The sun had sunk to the horizon, and the branches of the trees were silhouetted against the gray of the sky.

"I don't actually care what you remember to think about." Devon's voice was low and tense. "It's mine, and I'm keeping it."

I snapped my eyes shut, willing myself to fall back to sleep so I wouldn't be eavesdropping on my best friend.

"It's a magical object," Eric said.

"And I'm not magical so I don't deserve it?"

I slipped one eye open as a hum filled the air. Devon held the sword he had taken from The Game. Its red glow cut through the darkness, making the bare branches of the trees look like bloody fingers scratching the night in their fury to kill us. I squeezed my eyes shut again.

"It isn't about deserving," Eric said. "It's about safety."

"And you don't think I can handle a sword? I seem to remember chopping a guy's hand off while saving you a few hours ago."

"And I am eternally grateful for your assistance."

Devon made a noise somewhere between a *tsh* and a *growl*.

"I don't think a derring-do like yourself should be given an inconsistent magical object they can take into battle."

"I've fought with you twice now," Devon said coldly.

I wanted to smack Eric on the head and warn him that *when Devon uses that voice, either say he's right and apologize, or run for your life.* Those were the only two options available.

"I've stood in the middle of magical battles with nothing to defend myself. And it never once occurred to you that maybe you should mention magical light sabers exist? Or what about the tray shields the non-human bussers had? Do I not merit a way to fight? To defend myself and the people I care about? Am I just supposed to stand around being disposable?"

"I would never dream of calling you disposable—"

"But I am."

"What you are is one who has walked into dangerous magic and survived based purely on self-confidence and an inability to recognize danger," Eric spoke quickly as though trying to make sure Devon didn't interrupt. "What you are is someone who seems to place his own mortality at an extraordinarily low priority when protecting others."

"That's really rich coming from you."

"But I can defend myself," Eric said. "My magic is consistent. I can count on it. When I go into danger, I know exactly what my defenses are and how far they can be pushed. That sword is an enchanted object."

"An enchanted object that saved our lives," Devon jumped in.

"I'll give you that," Eric conceded. "But next time you need it, the sword could fail. Imbuing objects with magic is a tetchy thing. They can falter without cause. The spell can shift without warning. And it would leave you running into battle thinking you have a sword and ending up with a paperweight. I never told you such things exist, because I prefer to keep those around me alive."

"And that's your prerogative?" Devon spat. "You get to keep us alive?"

"As the leader of this motley crew, it is my *duty*."

"And it's my *duty* to keep the people I care about safe." Devon's voice shifted, and the *thud* of pacing footsteps echoed around me. "Has it ever occurred to you that I know I might get killed? The battle in Beville, I was pretty sure I was gonna end up dead, but dying was better than abandoning my best friends. I'm scared shitless half the time. Everyone around me is doing magic and could kill me with a couple words, but I'm not going to leave the few people who actually matter to me in some underground world of weirdness and just hope I get to see them again."

"You have a family," Eric said. "You have a whole life aboveground. That isn't a thing you should so freely sacrifice."

"Bryant is my family."

His words hit me hard in the chest. I squeezed my eyes shut to keep from crying.

"It's not like I have some great parents I'm ignoring to be here. Bryant and Elizabeth are the closest thing I have to a warm fuzzy family." Devon's voice dropped. "You've said it before— we're all in this together. I get that you all have these awesome powers that make you a part of magic. But I'm a part of it, too. Because I can't live with letting any of you get hurt. I can't survive standing on the sidelines while people I care about are in danger. That's a million times worse than getting hurt."

"Or killed?" Eric asked, his voice gentle.

"Or killed."

Tears leaked from my eyes.

"And here I thought you were simply incapable of fear."

"I spend half my life terrified." Devon gave a dry laugh. "I'm just scared of different things."

"Keep the sword." There was a shuffling on the ground like someone standing up. "And I'll find someone to fashion you a few more treats if we survive long enough to get back to Beville."

"Thank you."

"But please remember, Devon, fate can choose to twist magic in strange ways to fit her will. Twisting the magic in that sword would be an easy task for her."

"I know."

The urge to jump up, hug my best friend, steal the sword from him, and lock him in a safe room was overwhelming. But I knew Devon well enough to know he was right. Not being able to help was a worse fate for him than being hurt. And it was my job to make sure he didn't get so hurt we couldn't heal him.

20

"Time to begin." Eric's words were a relief since I had been lying there pretending to sleep for who knew how long.

Darkness had fallen in earnest now. Streetlamps lit the wide path even though there were no tourists to be seen, and bright beams of light shone on the Statue of Liberty.

"Was it some sort of feminist thing?" Devon asked lightly, all traces of his talk with Eric brushed away.

"I'm not sure I understand. *Nudla*," Eric said, and his coat was drycleaner-fresh with a tiny *hiss*.

"The Ladies chose their emergency exit from the Library to be at Lady Liberty." Devon brushed his coat off by hand.

I gave my coat a firm shake and used the same spell Eric had. The grass disappeared, but it didn't get the nice pressed lines on the sleeves Eric's had.

"More a matter of convenience, I think, though admittedly I've never asked." With a wave of Eric's hand, the shield around us disappeared. "This island is far enough away from the city to be safe in case of an attack, isolated enough to give some semblance of privacy, and nowhere that the exit could be stumbled upon accidentally."

"But how many tourists swarm over this island every day?" Elizabeth said.

I turned to ask if she wanted me to clean her coat, but she already looked perfect. I was so distracted by the swish of her skirt I didn't realize the others were cutting through the trees until Elizabeth almost slipped out of sight.

"The island is frequently invaded by tourists," Eric said once I jogged to catch up, like he had known I had fallen behind while marveling over the wonderment of my girlfriend. "But the entrance isn't on the island."

"Then please tell me there's a good reason we've been sitting here for hours," Devon said, his hand firmly in his pocket as we cut through the shadows. I had a strong gut feeling he was grasping his sword.

"Other than a nice rest in the fresh air?" Eric said. "Of course. The Library exit isn't on the island." He stopped at the edge of the water. "It's beneath it."

I scanned the beach, hoping for a hidden door to pop open or even for a chasm to appear. But Eric just stared at the mucky, nasty water.

"We have to get in the Hudson?" Elizabeth asked, revulsion sounding in her voice. It wasn't hard to see why.

The filth of the Hudson sloshed up against the shore of the perfectly manicured island. Plastic bottles floated next to rotting garbage. The whole thing was topped off with one distended, dead rat.

"You have got to be kidding me." I swallowed hard, trying not to hurl at the thought of swimming next to the dead rat and making a silent vow that if we lived through the night, I would really work on getting a stronger stomach for grossness. "There is no way anyone would swim next to that. Let alone the Ladies who fancy pure white fashion."

"Many wonderful things in this world are hidden right

beneath the horrible. It's one of the safest places to be." Eric leaned toward the water, apparently unfazed by Devon, Elizabeth, and me glaring, horrorstruck, at his back. "It's quite simple, really. We dive in here and swim down. You'll see the entrance when you get close to it. Swim right in. There will be air waiting in the light."

"Swim toward the light." Elizabeth's voice trembled. "Great."

"I'll hop in first as a show of good faith. Best not to think about it too much." Eric stepped out to the ledge, and in one swift movement dove into the river, disappearing beneath the dark water.

"Lovely." Devon wiped his hands over his face. "I'd say ladies first but that would be cruel. See you on the other side."

Pulling himself up to his full height, he lifted his arms and dove into the water.

"Me next." Elizabeth stepped toward the ledge.

"I can go," I said. The thought of her having to swim through the muck was almost worse than doing it myself.

"If I go, you'll dive right in." Elizabeth smiled at me. "You wouldn't let me swim into the dark alone, would you?"

Then she was gone. She dove in like it was nothing. Like freezing water and dead rats were nothing to worry about. Like cancer-causing, flesh-eating diseases weren't in every drop of nasty river touching Elizabeth's perfect eyes and flooding into her dainty nose.

With a forceful kick, her heeled shoes sank out of sight.

It was my turn.

I took a deep breath, trying not to think of the bacteria I would soon be submerged in that was probably going to kill me before the Ladies ever got a chance. The current had pushed all the garbage right up next to the shore, so if I jumped far enough, I might be able to clear it and not actually touch the distended rat. I raised my arms like Devon had...and dove.

Well, tried to dive. It was more like falling a few feet from shore and belly-flopping into the water. The impact knocked the air out of my lungs, and river water flooded my mouth. I gagged and retched, but I couldn't even cough. It was too cold pull in any air. The rat had been stirred back into the current by my belly flop. He was missing one eye, and the horrible void glared at me as he drifted closer.

I gasped for air and dove, kicking and hoping it was only my imagination as something brushed against my ankle. I swam down into the cold. Certain I was going to die. The freezing water, the current, something was going to get me. I wasn't going to die in an epic battle. I was going to drown in the Hudson. A jogger would find my body. The police would come, and they would probably rule my death a suicide.

I swam down farther, and my lungs started to burn. Pressure surged in my ears. My whole head was bound to explode. The water was too dark to see any of the others.

Pain seared my lungs.

Would my lungs pop first or my head?

Maybe I had swum the wrong way and the others would all survive. They would be able to tell my mom what happened.

If they survived the Ladies.

The current of the river caught my coat, dragging me backward, or what seemed like backward. There was no light for me to fight toward. Nothing left but darkness.

My arms burned as the weight of my wet wool coat became too much. A new current grabbed me, dragging me farther down. Farther away from the air I so desperately needed.

Lights danced in front of my eyes.

Please let the others be okay.

More than anything I wanted to stop. To let the freezing water squeeze me into nothing so the pain would end. But I couldn't. I had to fight as long as I could to get to them. To help them survive. I owed all of them that.

The lights got brighter, burning my eyes.

No, not lights. One light. One impossibly bright light.

I was only seeing one bright white light.

I kicked as hard as I could, using my very last bit of strength and fell, heaving, onto a white marble floor.

21

"Bryant," a beautiful angel called my name. "Bryant!" The angel was mad. "Bryant, wake up!" The angel smacked me.

"Ow!" I coughed. Water tumbled from my mouth.

"Oh thank God!" The angel was Elizabeth, and she pulled me into her soaking wet, foul-smelling arms.

Devon sank to the ground next to me, his whole body shaking, his face a mixture of exhaustion and relief.

"You okay?" I asked him. My voice came out all raspy like I'd gotten overly enthusiastic at a football game.

"I'm good." Devon nodded, flopping his hair into his eyes.

"I told you we would all make it." Eric was not hovering worriedly over me. He stood away from us on the other side of the white room.

All four walls were made out of the same pure white marble as the floor. There were no lights in the room, just a warm, ambient glow that seemed to come from nowhere in particular. The only break in the stone was the ceiling, which was made of river. The surface of the water wasn't visible. But the river flowed over us as though we were sitting under a giant fish tank. But there was no glass. I should know—I'd just fallen through that ceiling.

"Where are we?" I struggled to my feet.

"At the exit of the Library." Eric turned an appraising eye toward me. "Did you hit your head?"

"I mean *how* are we here?" I pointed up to the water, pushing down the horrible feeling it was going to spill onto our heads at any moment and crush us all to death.

"Magic." Eric shrugged, turning back to the white wall in front of him.

"Thanks," I grumbled.

"I've told you before, breaking into the Library is dangerous." Eric ran his fingers along the marble like a pianist playing on invisible keys. "I need you all to do exactly what I say, exactly when I say it. There will be no room for argument. No time to second-guess my decisions. We're waltzing into the best security system known to magickind. If you move one hair out of my guidance, I cannot guarantee you will live to see the inside of the Library."

"And if we do everything you say?" I asked.

"Then I still can't promise your survival." Eric's fingers stopped, hovering a centimeter over the stone. "But I will feel terrible for a long time that you died a horrific death. Everyone ready?"

"Can't we get dry first?" Elizabeth asked through chattering teeth.

"No point." Eric pressed his fingers to the wall.

A *pop* sounded high above us followed by a *hiss* and a *slam*.

I looked up in time to see a thick panel of glass slide into place on the ceiling.

"We're trapped," I whimpered as water trickled into our cell from the edges of the glass.

"Not entirely." Eric's voice was calm enough to pull my horrified gaze from the falling water. He had stepped out of the room. Sort of.

A thin veil of mist separated him from the rest of us. And where he was standing wasn't flooding at the same alarming rate as the rest of the chamber. I slogged through the knee-high water toward him with Devon and Elizabeth close behind me. I dove toward the translucent wall and hit something hard with my face.

"Eric, let us in!" Elizabeth pounded on the mist, and a reverberating *thud* echoed around the room.

"Not yet, Elizabeth." Eric faced away from us, doing something I couldn't see. He swirled his hands through the air like a painter working top speed on a giant canvas.

"The water's getting high out here!" Devon shouted a few seconds later when the water reached our waists.

"I'm doing rather delicate work." The annoyance in Eric's voice wasn't as terrifying as the undertone of fear.

"We have to go back up." Devon turned away from Eric to the glass ceiling above us. "My sword might cut through it."

"It won't work," Eric said.

"Well, I'm not going to let us die out here!" Devon shouted.

"There is nothing you can do," Eric said.

I had followed a psychopath, and now we were going to be human sacrifices to buy his way into the Library.

Maybe that was how he got in the first time. Maybe it had been his plan from the beginning.

The water was up to our shoulders. Devon flicked his sword on and held it up toward the ceiling. The burning red blade was a few inches shy of reaching the glass.

"Elizabeth." I turned to her to say something deep and meaningful about how being with her was better than magic.

But Elizabeth didn't look at me. She was staring through the mist at Eric, watching him slice his hands through the air like she could actually see what he was doing.

"Elizabeth, what is it?" I asked as the water lifted me off my feet.

"Come on, come on," Elizabeth murmured, treading water.

"Elizabeth, what is he doing?" I shouted.

"Saving us."

The mist dissolved with a *whoosh*. The water surrounding us shot up toward the ceiling, like we were being attacked by a giant with a Shop-Vac. Each drop tore at my skin as it was sucked away. My hair hurt from being yanked toward the river. And then we fell. I hit the marble floor just as hard as I had a few minutes before and grunted as someone landed on top of me.

"Ouch," Elizabeth groaned as she rolled off of me.

"Are you serious!" Devon leapt to his feet. "Tell me you didn't know the room was going to flood."

"I'm perfectly happy to lie to you whenever you like," Eric said.

The mist separating him from us had disappeared, leaving an opening to a white tunnel in its place.

"We could have died!" Devon's shout echoed off the marble walls.

"Shh," Elizabeth hushed.

"We still might, and moving quickly is our best chance for making it to the Library alive," Eric said. "The hall won't remain open for long. If you'd like to come with me, I suggest we move quickly."

Elizabeth grabbed my hand and yanked me to my feet. Between the two near drowning experiences, my whole body shook. On the plus side, my clothes and hair were dry. And not like still sort of damp dry. Like creepy blow dryer dry.

"Come on." Elizabeth dragged me into the hall, pulling my

attention from my super dry clothes. "Devon!" Elizabeth snapped.

Devon hadn't moved. He was still standing in the white box, glaring at Eric. "And what if we get in there and lightning strikes us? Or swords pop out of the walls and skewer us?"

"Stop being dramatic," Eric said. "We don't have time for it. You knew this was dangerous long before we dove into the water."

"But I didn't think we would be lied to!" Devon shouted. "After everything we've been through, you just walk through some mist and leave us to tread water. We are not pawns. We are the closest thing to friends you have. Friends don't abandon their friends."

"I wasn't abandoning you." Eric stepped out of the hall and reached toward Devon. "I promise I'll explain, but we have to go now. Or we will be abandoning Bryant and Elizabeth in the Library with no hope of survival."

"We have to go," Elizabeth warned, staring at where the wall had been.

Squinting, I could kind of make out a subtle solidifying of the air in the corners.

"Now, guys!"

"I really hate you sometimes," Devon growled and ran for the hall. A sound like breaking glass came at the same instant he faltered. A cut appeared on his cheek as he charged forward, Eric on his heels.

"What was that?" Devon wiped blood from his cheek.

"The wall regrowing," Elizabeth answered.

"It's a failsafe door to get into the library." Eric beckoned us farther down the hall while the white room with the square of Hudson hovering above disappeared behind a very solid, white wall. "You have to find the door, which is no mean feat, and everyone locked in the chamber has to perform the spell. A spell none of you are capable of."

"How does he know that?" I whispered to the solid white marble ceiling above. The ceiling didn't answer, which I was really happy about.

"Is that what all the hand flapping was?" Devon asked, his tone still angry.

"The use of arrow magic is arcane," Eric said.

The hall ate his voice, like the walls around us weren't solid and bare. The white corridor twisted off into the distance. The air lit with ambient light showed no marks or changes in the wall. It seemed too perfect, too harmless.

"It's an inconsistent branch of magic. One misplaced arch of the finger and you could very well die. Its use fell out of favor a few centuries ago. I only bothered to track down its few living purveyors when I discovered arrow magic was necessary to enter the Library. The only firsthand accounts of failed attempts to enter the Library I've heard are those of the people who stayed where the water floods in the first chamber.

"That portion is possible to break out of. I met more than one unfortunate soul who lost their compatriots to the mist in the arrow magic chamber. It's funny," Eric paused, "the Ladies who guard the books use magic that can't be written to guard them. It's almost as if they don't trust the books themselves."

A shiver prickled the back of my neck as Eric laughed like he had just told a wonderful joke.

"So you left us to drown because you needed to use out-of-date magic to pick a magical lock?" Devon asked. "That was you protecting us?"

"Exactly." Eric nodded and started back down the hall.

"And what near death are you tossing us into next?" Devon asked.

"It's not tossing, more of a sprinting wiggle," Eric said.

"What?" Devon growled between gritted teeth.

"Yeah, I concur with the *what*," I panted. We were only moving at a speedy walk, but the fear of whatever was coming next, combined with all the almost dying of the day, was confusing the hell out of my fight-or-flight reflexes.

"The Ladies were very smart," Eric said. "They didn't use one sort of barricade to block the exit. The arrow magic, the cogs, the chasm. All patterns the Ladies would easily know how to solve, which are exponentially easier going the opposite direction than we are currently traveling."

"Okay, so we swam the river, got past the arrow thing." My voice sounded annoyingly optimistic, even to me. "Now we just have to do the cogs and the chasm. That makes us, like, halfway there."

A faint grinding sound drifted from down the hall where the walls swerved to one side, hiding whatever the moving thing was from view.

"Theoretically," Eric said, pulling my focus from the sound.

"Whoa, whoa, what do you mean *theoretically*?" Devon asked.

"That's as far as I made it."

22

The grinding sound was overpowering even before the gateway came into view. The ceiling of the tunnel sloped upward to reach the top of a high arch. Sparkling silver bars covered the opening, obscuring my view of the moving things beyond.

"There really isn't much I can tell you about this." Eric squinted through the shining bars. "Keep up, don't touch anything, don't get crushed. If I ask you to do something, assume it's for your survival."

Devon rolled his eyes.

"Isn't that you wanted me to do?" Eric asked. "Give you an honest representation of what to expect?"

"Let's just go." Devon reached for the bars.

I expected Eric to stop him or for Devon to be electrocuted and die, but he grabbed the gate and swung it open.

My brain froze, trying to comprehend what was happening. It looked like the inside of a clock. If the clock were magical and massive.

Cogs with shifting shapes latched onto one another, moving sideways, pulling each other toward the unseeable ceiling or mashing themselves between other moving bits. Some of the cogs didn't appear to be totally solid. They would grow and shrink as they moved from one gap to another.

And the patterns on them—giant geometric shapes shimmered as they twisted around the surfaces, and smaller markings, like a language beyond my comprehension, floated in and out of view.

"There's no way through it," I said as the others stepped into the room.

"What's your problem?" Elizabeth whispered to Devon as Eric moved into the lead.

"Nothing," Devon murmured.

"Dev."

"I can't take partial trust," Devon answered barely loudly enough for me to hear over the cogs. "Either we're all in this together, or I'm not in it at all. I'm done being treated like a bystander or a child. I'm neither of those things."

Elizabeth opened her mouth to speak, but Devon had already walked away.

"The trick is to not get crushed to death while moving the cogs into the right position to free the path forward." Eric stood at center of the space, glowering at the cogs around him.

"It's like a puzzle." Elizabeth stepped in front of him. "Each of the patterns complements another, and if you put them together right..."

It was like she was in a trance. Two giant wheels wound around each other, their jagged, angular patterns not seeming to have any relation. Elizabeth reached forward, pressing her fingers through the air as though meshing the cogs together. But there was nothing there to mesh, only giant things that were going to suck her in and kill my girlfriend.

"Elizabeth, no!" I lunged forward a second too late. Her hands met stone.

The stone wheels shifted, and my heart stopped for a moment. But they didn't mash Elizabeth, because they weren't turning toward each other anymore. They were twisting and opening up, creating five little cogs that only took up half the space the two large ones had.

"I really did hope you were going to have a talent for this," Eric said with as close to a broad smile as I think he was capable of.

"The pattern made sense." Elizabeth blushed.

"I don't know of any seers who have tried to make it through the cogs, or at least not any who survived the attempt." Eric turned back to the wheels. "I had hoped your skills would translate to this particular task, but there was really no way to know. I could have done it myself." Eric approached a set of three cogs. One sat on the bottom and narrowed at the top, allowing the two great wheels to push it around and around. "I did it before, after all. But I was stuck in this room for three days before I managed to find the way forward."

"Three days!" I coughed.

"Yes." Eric leapt forward, grabbing a part of the pattern and twisting it sideways, creating a perfect set of parallel lines that spanned all three moving parts. The bottom cylinder dropped away, leaving a gap where it had been. "And we really don't have three days."

"So what should we be looking for?" Devon asked, his face betraying the same confusion I felt.

"I'm not sure either of you will be able to see it." Elizabeth didn't look away from the spire that swirled up and down from the floor. "It's like there's a missing piece to each of them. A place they belong they can't quite reach on their own. And you have to...." She threw herself forward, knocking the spire sideways where it kept turning, rotating a bit of the puzzle I hadn't even noticed before.

"Okay." Devon searched the cogs. "Okay."

"Please don't, Devon," Eric said, his tone kinder than usual. "The pattern is incredibly intricate and difficult to find. One wrong move, and things could go very badly."

Devon froze for a moment, his face somewhere between stone and demon killer. "Fine. The simple human will stay out of the way."

"I think this is one." Elizabeth pointed high above our heads to where five strands of the ceiling pulled in different directions, apparently oblivious to Devon looking like mutiny was in his near future.

Not leaving Devon's side, I stared up at the ceiling. Each of the strips had a different pattern on it, one like sweeping hills, another like binary code.

"There has to be a way it fits together," Elizabeth murmured. "How did you do it last time you were here?"

"Quite frankly, the entire room was different." Eric scowled. "I can't be sure, of course, but I feel like you could make it into this room a hundred times and never find the puzzle to be quite the same. You simply have to figure it out."

Eric jabbed a set of tiny cogs I hadn't even noticed. That portion of the wall came to a screeching halt.

Carefully, Eric pulled a gold cog from the pattern and carried it across the room. He glared at the wall for a moment, then inserted the cog into a crack barely large enough for it to slip through.

The floor shuddered as those bits of the puzzle shifted out of sight.

"Now we're getting somewhere," Eric said, his tone thick with concentration. "Elizabeth, keep an eye on the ceiling, if you will."

Eric stepped into the gap the last move had made as the wall he had stolen the cog from came back to life, moving in a completely different way than it had before.

"We're inside a lock," I whispered to Devon. "We're inside a giant lock, and they're twisting the tumblers by hand."

"You mean *you all* are." Devon's face was still stony.

"I don't see any of it." I shook my head in awe as Eric swiped a column forcing it to turn faster. The wall behind us twisted, and the floor shuddered again.

"I'm sure you will," Devon said. "Just look at it, and you'll see something great. A spell you have to do. Something amazing for you to accomplish."

"Devon." I took a deep breath. Devon was my best friend. Had been my best friend for years. But deep and meaningful conversations weren't things we did very often. "I know what it's like to feel useless."

"So I'm useless." Devon didn't even sound mad. "A useless kid to be led by the hand through the scary world of magic."

"No," I said quickly, "you aren't. You're a brave badass. What I'm saying is just because magic and seeing aren't your thing doesn't mean we don't need you. The number of times you've saved me proves it. We need you—I need you—just the way you are."

"Dammit, Bry. Are we in a chick flick now?" Devon smiled, not like a giddy smile, but it was something. "Good to know my utter normalness is handy."

"You have a sword, dude." I laughed. "My best friend has a magic sword. I think that's pretty—"

The floor gave another shudder, sharper and more violent than before.

"Oh no." Elizabeth stepped back from the far wall, which was much farther away than it had been when I'd stopped paying attention a few minutes before.

I scanned Elizabeth for signs of injury or impending death. She looked fine except for the horror on her face.

"Miss Wick." Eric leapt back into view.

"I thought I'd found one." Elizabeth's hands flew to her mouth, and the wall whirred. It was still turning like it was a part of the puzzle, but the whirring had changed. The tone of it was different. Dangerous.

"Everyone this way!" Eric dove toward the opening he'd made in the cogs.

I sprinted the few feet to follow him as Elizabeth dove into the gap.

A hand shoved me forward and I fell to the floor the second before a bright light flashed behind us and Eric bellowed, "*Primurgo!*"

Heat nipped at my back for a moment before the light dissipated.

"Devon!" I gasped, pushing myself off the ground.

"Human's alive," Devon panted from just inside the shield.

I slumped back onto my elbows.

"Everyone intact?" Eric asked, his pale face shining with sweat.

Elizabeth whimpered. "I thought I was helping. I'm so sorry."

"You are helping, Elizabeth." Eric let go of the shield and stepped over me. "Helping doesn't mean perfection. But please don't make another mistake. The punishment will only be worse."

"Right." Elizabeth nodded, smoothing out her skirt. "No more mistakes."

Devon helped me to my feet as Elizabeth leaned in to examine a gear twice the size of my head.

The cog room was just the same as when we had fled from it a minute before. No signs of fire or exploding death.

"I think I found one," Elizabeth called.

"If you're sure, then do it." Eric stood staring up at the ceiling.

Elizabeth muttered a long string of curses and twisted a tiny hinge. From the shaking of the floor and the widening of the gap, she had been right.

"We should be nearly there." Eric pointed up to the ceiling. "Look how it's changed. The speed, the variation. Everything we do alters the pattern above. It's symbolic—it almost makes sense."

"Almost?" I asked.

"*Almost* can mean quite a bit when dealing with magic."

"Going to try another one," Elizabeth said. "Promise to miss me if I die?"

"Elizabeth, that's not funny." I spun to face her, and my heart leapt into my throat as she stuck her hand into a portion of the wall that looked like a giant jaw ready to chomp my girlfriend's arm off. "Elizabeth!"

She twisted her arm quickly, reaching up inside the jaw, and wrenched her arm back, yanking on something.

The jaw froze, and she pulled her hand away as the wall crumbled into nothing. The floor shook, but not in an evil *gonna kill you* kind of way, more like a *janky turntable on a stage* kind of way.

A *clang* shook the far wall as the gate we had passed through swung shut.

Devon ran forward and rattled the gate.

"Trapped is better than dead?" Elizabeth shrugged.

"We're nearly there," Eric whispered to the ceiling.

"And how do we get there?" I asked.

The room had gotten larger. None of the moving pieces I'd first seen were still there, and I still didn't have any idea what I was supposed to be looking for. If I tilted my head sideways and really focused, I could tell the movements were different. It wasn't a thousand pieces of a hundred puzzles. It had evolved into one giant puzzle with a few pieces just slightly out of place.

"I don't see anything else." Elizabeth stared frantically from one wall to the next. "I don't see anything else to change."

And then I did something stupid/brilliant. I closed my eyes.

It was a game I used to play when I was little and scared of the dark. If you can't see the monsters, try to hear them coming. All it had accomplished was instilling a healthy fear of Mrs. Mops, but that's beside the point.

Squeezing my eyes shut, I listened to the hum of the room. The grinding and whirring of the cogs had changed with every switch in the walls. The new tone was brighter, as though there were less density for the sound to fight through. But a lower buzz still rumbled from the left corner.

"Over there." I pointed like an auditory divining rod. "The change needs to be made over there."

"What?" Elizabeth said. "Where?"

"I don't know." I moved over to that side of the room, squinting at the squares that rotated like a Rubik's cube. "But it's something here."

Elizabeth squinted at the squares as they clinked together, switching between silver, gold, and shining white. "Here." Elizabeth reached her hand forward. "No here."

"You do know you really need to be right, right?" Devon whispered over my shoulder.

"Not helping." Elizabeth's hand shook as she reached forward. "Really not helping." With a quick swipe, she struck the square the instant five whites lined up. "Bingo," Elizabeth breathed.

The floor shook again as the squares smoothed out. The wall, still covered in cogs, gears, and moving parts, had pushed back so it was almost like we were standing in a square room.

"And here we have it," Eric said from the center of the room.

The pattern on the ceiling had changed yet again. The middle three strips moved one way at three different speeds while the outer two moved in the other direction at the same pace, like tracks made by the wheels of the car.

"Anyone have a stick to poke it?" I asked.

"Devon, lift Elizabeth," Eric said casually.

"Plié on three." Devon took Elizabeth's hips. "One, two, down, up."

In one smooth motion, she popped up to sit on his shoulder. My mom would be thrilled dance classes had yet another practical application.

"Slow the center," Eric said.

Elizabeth reached up and dragged her fingers along the center strip, slowing the speed. Without waiting for further instruction, she swiped her hand along the second strip like she was spinning a roulette wheel, doubling its speed.

"You're going the wrong way." Elizabeth dug her fingers into the third strip and flung it the other direction.

A picture appeared, shimmering and moving in a breathtaking way. And at last, the pattern made beautiful sense. Waves drifted along the top of the water, with bubbles and froth surrounding the giant creatures swimming beneath.

I could have stood there watching for hours.

But a *clink* sounded, and the gate we had entered through swung open.

"No." Elizabeth slid down from Devon's shoulder. "No, no, no. We came from that way!"

"Not so quickly." Eric walked slowly toward the gate as though he still thought the room might chew us up.

"But we did come through that way." I followed Eric.

"We came through the gate, but it led someplace very different," Eric said.

"But how is that—" My protest at the impossibility of this magic disappeared.

We weren't in a shining, white hall. We were standing on the edge of a ravine seventy feet wide and so deep the bottom was lost in blackness.

"So how do we get across?" Devon asked.

"I have no idea," Eric said. "I never made it past."

23

"You never made it past?" I tested each of the words on my tongue to see where I might have gotten confused or slipped into an alternate reality.

"No." Eric glowered at the chasm as though the depth blocking his path were a personal affront.

"So you've fought shadows, mist Ladies, and magical kidnappers, and a hole in the ground stopped you?" My words came out more like a cry for help than a question.

"If you think you can do better, then please, go ahead," Eric said.

"No, I..." I stared at the endless pit of black, my insides freezing at the thought of it. "It just makes the hole sound really awful."

Devon chuckled behind me. "Evil hole of death."

"Okay," Elizabeth said bracingly, stepping up to the edge of the cliff and sliding her hand into mine. "You couldn't get across by yourself, but we're all here together now. The four of us together can work it out."

"That is my hope." Eric tented his fingers under his chin as he stared across the gap.

There was a doorway straight ahead of us, a silver gate like the one we had passed through moments before, but this one had glass set between each of the bars. Warm blue light filtered through the panes, and shadows drifted in and out of view.

"Uh, Eric," I whispered. "Are there people watching us?"

We all froze for a moment, watching the shapes twist behind the glass. It could have been flickering torchlight, or people waltzing...or the Ladies spinning in joy as they plotted our deaths.

"No," Eric said finally. "They did that for two days the last time I was here."

"You spent two days trying to cross this and failed?" Devon asked.

"It's more like shadows than actual people." Elizabeth cocked her head to the side, watching the glass.

"Shadows like *big bad evil* shadows?" I crossed the fingers on my free hand, hoping if there were monster shadows there wouldn't be a giant minotaur included.

"No, like shadows of things that have happened." Elizabeth shivered. "Eric, what's it like in the Library?"

"No idea. I've never been in it." Eric knelt and began crawling along the side of the cliff, trailing his fingers through the open air.

"There's no spell to fly across?" Elizabeth asked.

I pulled the black phone out of my pocket. The trip through the river had done no damage and the screen blinked on as soon as I pressed my thumb to the scanner. I'd spent countless hours in the past two months pouring over every app in the phone. Reading all the spells, trying to find a spare bit of brain to store them in. Making the spells a part of my magical knowledge base so I could use them without running into the rules of impartment the Ladies had created to stunt magical learning.

But nowhere had I found a spell for flying. It had been a

horrible disappointment. No enchanted brooms, no spell to sprout wings, not even a flying carpet.

"Flying isn't a thing wizards do," Eric said.

"Okay," Devon said. "What about throwing? You could throw each of us across. I mean you can move furniture, why not a person?"

"For many reasons," Eric said, not looking up as he scoured the ground, "but the short of it is no. That would still count as flying. I could hit you with a spell and hope it knocked you in the right direction, but that is a risk I'm not willing to take."

"But *escata* lets you kind of—"

Eric cut me off. "That is not flying, it's falling with style. I can assure you there is no possible way for you to fly over the gap and land undamaged on the other side."

"Great," Devon grumbled.

"Elizabeth, do you see anything of interest?" Eric asked.

Elizabeth took a long moment walking the edge of the chasm where Eric crawled, staring into the pit and over to the other side. "Nothing. As far as I can see it's just a deadly deep pit."

"Okay," I said, steeling myself to be brilliant. "These walls are made of rock, right?"

I was right. The walls that surrounded us weren't made of the glistening white marble of the halls. They were plain old rock like we had jumped into an Indiana Jones movie.

"So we use a spell to carve out a portion of the rock and magic it into a bridge." My words tumbled out. "Carve out a plank to lay across the crack."

"It won't work," Eric said, finally standing. "The rock can't be changed."

"But—"

"Feel free to try." Eric raised his hands placatingly.

I cringed, sure if he was so positive, this was obviously going to end badly for me, but we had to do something.

"*Caruson.*" I pointed at the wall like my finger was a knife ready to dig out stone. Pain shot through my finger, up my arm, and into my neck like I had just poked the third rail. "Gah!"

"You should have warned him." Elizabeth smacked Eric hard on the shoulder.

"I had to be sure it wouldn't work if someone else tried it." Eric shrugged.

"Maybe the way across is on the other side of the creepy glowing door." I rubbed the back of my neck, which stung like it had been attacked by bees. "Maybe there's a lever for a draw-bridge on the other side."

"Thaden got through," Eric said. "If he managed it, there's a way."

"He might have summoned demons from Hell to ferry him across," I said.

"Please be realistic, Bryant." Eric sighed, like of all the things I'd seen, mentioning demons from Hell was one step too far.

"Or he jumped," Devon said.

I turned toward him. He had been quiet for long enough that, being the horrible friend I am, I had lost track of him. Now he stood at the edge of the chasm, his toes a centimeter from the abyss.

"Somehow I doubt Thaden was suicidal," Eric said. "A leap like that would kill you."

"Bryant jumped out his bedroom window and lived." Devon didn't move away from the edge.

"My window was high." I took a slow step forward. "This could lead to China."

"Can you shine a light down and see how far it goes?" Elizabeth asked.

"The light just disappears," Eric said. "The pit is too deep for magic to penetrate."

"It's the only way forward. We have to try." Devon didn't look at us. He just stared into the pit.

"Supposing we were to jump and by some miracle we survived the fall. How would we get back out of the dark?" Eric asked. "Here we can get back out to the river. Down there we could starve to death."

"Not my fault you didn't pack snacks." Devon inched forward.

"Dev, this is crazy," Elizabeth said. "Even if Bryant and Eric could cushion the fall, I can't see what's waiting down there."

"That's the problem with you special people." Devon smiled. "You only see the magical ways. But when all other choices are gone, you only have the obvious path left. Forward means down." He moved forward an inch, spreading his arms wide.

"Devon!" I screamed, lunging toward him a second too late.

He tipped forward out of my grasp.

"*Escata!*" I screamed the spell, but Devon was falling too fast. Before the word had left my lips, Devon had been swallowed by the black.

I should have listened for a *thump* or a cry for help, but I couldn't stop myself from screaming. "Devon! Devon!"

"Devon!" Elizabeth's shout joined mine.

My best friend was dead. Devon. The brave one. The one with unbeatable suave and daring was dead. Lost forever. We wouldn't even have a body to bury.

I clasped my hands over my mouth to stop the terrible screams from coming. I didn't know I was crying until tears fell onto my fingers. He'd been my best friend since forever. Always there. Always Devon. Sobs banged in my chest. I'd never thought of not having Devon around. In all the madness, I never really thought I could lose him.

"Dev." Elizabeth knelt next to me, because somehow I was kneeling. I wrapped my arms around her, holding her as tight as I could, desperate not to lose her to the pit as well.

"Devon!" Eric called, his voice thoroughly lacking the utter horror of Devon's death. "Devon?"

"We should have grabbed him." Elizabeth coughed through her tears. "We should have found a way to stop him."

"Devon?" Eric called again. "Devon, can you hear us?"

"How could he hear us?" I jumped to my feet. "He's dead. My best friend in the world is dead. The closest thing I'll ever have to a brother—" I choked on the words as a fresh wave of tears took hold. "He was a better man than you'll ever be, and now he's dead. Don't be such a dick."

"Devon, have you had quite enough?" Eric asked.

"Quite enough? You son—"

Devon's voice cut me off. "Aww, come on." The words drifted up from the ravine.

No, not up—out.

"Can't a guy enjoy people crying and saying how wonderful he is?"

"Devon, where are you?" I called at the same moment Elizabeth shouted, "I'll kill you, Devon Rhodes!"

Devon walked out of the chasm on the other side. And I don't mean climbed, I mean walked. Stepped out of the black in the middle and walked onto the stone on the other side.

"What?" I sputtered. "How?"

"You knew he didn't die?" Elizabeth shrieked, punching Eric in the arm so hard he actually made a pained noise.

"I suspected." Eric rubbed his arm and stepped toward the edge.

"How?" Devon asked from across the chasm. "Because I didn't make a splatting noise?"

"The way the black swallowed you," Eric said, like we all

should have noticed the movement of the light while my best friend was jumping to his death. "It moved like you were jumping under something, not into something."

"Well, take the leap, folks." Devon spread his arms wide. "It's not too bad a fall."

"Devon Rhodes, I swear I am going to make you pay for this," Elizabeth growled as she stepped toward the edge.

"Me first." I stepped in front of her.

She raised one eyebrow at me in a shockingly Eric-like way.

"I don't think I can watch you fall," I said.

She brushed her fingers along my palm, and a tingle ran up my spine. Without taking a breath or thinking, I jumped.

I thought it would be a long fall. I thought air would *whoosh* past me, making my hair stand on end. But by the time I realized I had just jumped into a bottomless pit, I landed hard and fell forward in an awkward, gangly way. The landing didn't hurt much more than if I had jumped from the bleachers at school. It didn't feel nice, but I was on my feet in a second.

"Bryant?" Elizabeth shouted. "Are you okay?"

"I'm fine!" I looked up at where I had jumped from. The edge of the cliff was distorted, looking both too far away and too close at the same time. A few feet out from the edge a solid ceiling of black began, and on the other side was another gap, this one clearer with Devon waving me over.

It only took me a few seconds to walk across the invisible black floor beneath me. I took a breath preparing for a jump up, but when I stepped toward Devon I was just...on the other side.

"See? Not so bad." Devon beamed.

I took a page from Elizabeth's book and punched him in the shoulder.

"And you just thought it would be fun to not tell us you weren't jumping to your death?" I averted my eyes as Elizabeth jumped. "How the hell did you know you weren't going to splat?"

"I didn't." Devon shrugged. "I mean not *for sure* for sure. But it was what we had to try, so one of us was going to have to do it. We can't go back from this, Bry. We aren't here on a leisurely pleasure trip. We're here because the Ladies want all of us dead. Because creepy Kendrick McDonald wants us dead and you in a cage. We can't afford to fail. That would mean bad people and death."

"But that doesn't mean you get to jump!" I tore my hands through my hair. "I get that it's hard, and I get that we have to do this, but that doesn't mean you can charge into something stupid without the rest of us. We're a team. We need you. And not as a guinea pig for deadly things. No more risks, Devon."

The smile slid from Devon's face. "You know how you had to jump before Elizabeth? That's the way I feel about you. All of you. I can't watch people get hurt, Bry. Not when I can stop it. I just don't have it in me."

Elizabeth emerged from the chasm like she was just walking out of a shadow. She nailed Devon in the shoulder and pulled him into a hug. "I'm so mad at you right now."

"Good to see you, too." Devon's smile slid back into place.

Eric walked out of the dark. "That was surprisingly pleasant, all things considered." He dusted off his jacket, making sure a stray piece of filth hadn't marred his perfection. Because that sort of thing matters when you're breaking into a magical library.

"So now what?" I asked, staring at the gate. A silver handle melded seamlessly into the bars, like it was just an ordinary door that happened to glow all magical and blue.

"I believe we should open it." Eric reached toward the handle.

"And if all sorts of monsters jump out at us?" Elizabeth whispered.

"Then I suggest Mr. Rhodes get out his sword."

The blue glass of the door reflected the red light of Devon's sword as a faint hum sounded behind me.

I held my breath as Eric turned the handle and the gate swung open, bathing us all in bright blue light.

24

I don't know what I expected, but as I stood there blinking, I knew this wasn't it. Deep blue light flooded the air, just as the white light had done before, cutting shadows deep into the divots and niches of the roughly hewn stone walls. There were no people or even monsters waiting for us beyond the gate, but I couldn't shake the feeling there was something *there*. I don't even know if I can describe the feeling of knowing there are a hundred eyes staring at you and knowing those eyes don't exist at the same time.

"What is this place?" I whispered, following Eric into the blue light.

"Are you sure we should be here?" Elizabeth asked.

"Of course we shouldn't. That's the point." Even Eric kept his voice low.

A *creak* and a dull *thud* made me gasp and spin around as the blue door swung shut.

"Check the knob," I whispered, proud my voice didn't sound like I was about to poop my pants.

Thankfully, the knob turned easily.

"No point in locking the emergency exit." A laugh wobbled in my throat, completely blowing my cool act.

"We should keep moving." Elizabeth took my hand, not in a girlfriend way, but in a *for the love of all that is holy, don't leave me alone here* kind of way.

"I wholeheartedly agree." Eric stepped farther into the hall.

"I don't see any books," I whispered as we reached the first nook. Peering into the shadows in the niche, there were no book spines or even scrolls to be found.

But there was a shape floating in the shadows. Bone white with gaping black holes for eyes.

"Skull!" I scampered to the other side of the hall, dragging Elizabeth with me, but the opposite niche held another skull. This one missing teeth.

"This isn't a Library, Eric." Devon held up his sword, its red glow making the skull look even more terrifying.

"I didn't know where they put them." Eric reached out and caressed the skull. "They've all just been taken." He leaned down, speaking to the skull. "You must have been someone very important."

"Eric, explain right now," Elizabeth snapped.

"We've found the catacombs." Eric looked up, excitement and wonder lighting his eyes. "I've always wanted to see them, and here they are, hidden right along with the Library."

"So we are still aiming for the Library?" I asked.

"Of course. That is the mission," Eric answered.

"Just checking." I held my free hand up. Elizabeth clung to my other hand so tightly, I couldn't have let go even if I'd wanted to. Not that I'm complaining.

"Who are, I mean, *were* these people?" Devon leaned in close to one of the skulls. "Is it like Merlin or something?"

"Possibly. It could be any number of truly incredible people."

Eric spoke reverently, something I wasn't used to from him. "It could be my grandmother for all I know."

"But what are they doing here?" Devon asked. "I mean, I was sort of kidding. If Merlin did exist, wouldn't he be buried in England somewhere?"

"At one point." Eric stepped slowly away from the niche. "We should keep moving. We're in the Library now. We've no way to be certain they went to tidy up the mess at The Game. And even if fate favored us with their departure, they could come back at any moment." He turned and walked down the hallway.

I hoped it would just be a few skulls of famous dead witches and wizards and then done, but no such luck. They just kept going on and on. Some of the niches were small, just large enough to fit a solitary skull. Others were massive with ornate pedestals holding up the bones. A wide alcove held a base of carved gold with an inscription on it in some language that didn't use our alphabet. I teetered on the edge of asking Eric if he knew what the words said, but I didn't want to linger with the skulls for a second more than necessary.

"I still don't understand why there are skulls in a library," Elizabeth said when we reached the first full skeleton. All the bones floated in midair with no visible supports. It was like a living person was standing in the coffin-sized hole in the wall, but all their tissue and squishy bits were invisible.

"When you spend your life in magic, the magic itself starts to seep into you," Eric said softly. I wasn't sure if he was afraid of disturbing the dead or of the Ladies coming after us. "A dead witch or wizard's bones hold power."

I audibly gagged.

"Not for any sort of magic you would be interested in, Bryant." Eric glanced back over his shoulder. "Try not to desecrate this sacred place with your vomit."

"Sorry," I muttered.

"Most bone magic is done by humans who are trying to find a way into the magical world," Eric continued. "Only the darkest of wizards would dare use another wizard's magic after his death."

"A dark wizard like Thaden?" Devon asked.

"Exactly like Thaden," Eric said. "Which might explain how he became so very strong toward the end. If he stole bones and words, he made himself nearly invincible."

"The nearly part is very lucky for us," I whispered.

We passed a hollowed out area larger than the ones we had seen before, but shorter too. Three skeletons barely as tall as my shoulder hovered an inch above the ground, all holding boney hands. My brain couldn't decide between thinking it was beautiful or demonic.

"Are they like, from Salem?" Devon whispered.

"Possibly." Eric leaned in to give the bones a closer look. "If I had time to examine them I might be able to learn more."

"And this is why we need placards and docents," I murmured.

An archway loomed in the distance. I said a silent prayer to whoever was willing to listen to wizards on a breaking and entering spree that nothing to do with death would be on the other side of that arch. Either lots of dead people or us getting killed. Both would have been terrible options.

"My God." Eric ran into the next room.

"Eric." I ran after him. It only took me a second to see the thing he had seen that I instantly wished I had never seen.

Piles and piles of bones. Not jumbled up, but laid out in patterns. Long leg bones arranged in sturdy stacks to support a sea of skulls.

"How many in this room have I met?" Eric's hand shook as he reached out to touch a skull.

The weight of it all suddenly settled in my chest. All these people were the ones who had come before me. I may not have a blood relation to any wizards, but these were the ones who mined for the spells that were the language that gave me power. These people had created Beville and built the Library. These were my people.

It felt like the whole Hudson had poured down on my body. I couldn't breathe, I couldn't think. The weight of centuries of magic smothered me. I only knew I needed to get out.

"We need to go," I panted, not caring if I looked like a coward. "We have to get out of here."

Taking the lead, I stumbled down the row of skulls and shinbones. I ran the length of a city block before the tunnel twisted. A brief moment of relief lifted the weight from my lungs, but around the corner was just another long line of bones.

Trapped. I'm going to be trapped forever. Literally forever. My bones will just join the pile.

I broke into a full out run. Vaguely, I heard voices behind me telling me to come back, but I didn't want to be trapped in the deep blue light forever. The tunnel swerved into another corridor. A section of this bone wall had collapsed, leaving skulls scattered on the floor. I leapt over jawbones—which had detached from their craniums and were strewn on the ground—like I was playing hopscotch with death.

The crumbled section of broken skulls showed what was behind. A jumble of ribs, vertebrae, and other bones I never knew the names of. I leapt over the bones, desperate to get away. My foot skidded on a shinbone, and I hit the floor, smacking my head on the stone.

Not bothering to check if I was bleeding, I scrambled to my feet and kept running. Around another corner to a small room, where the bones were laid out in a fancy pattern, long bones crisscrossing around skulls. Words had been engraved high on the wall. *Honor those who bled.*

I was incapable of thinking about who might have bled, because there was no blood left. No pulses or hearts. Just bones. An impossible sea of bones.

All I could do was run.

Around the next corner the light changed. The blue filtered out, and a warm, normal looking glow called from the end of the hall.

A carved archway, thicker and fancier than any I had seen before, surrounded the exit. Words I didn't understand were inscribed in the stone. For a spilt second, I thought the archway would collapse, trapping me with the bones forever. Leaving me to starve to death.

I dove through the arch, like it was a closing hatch in an action movie, and skidded to a halt on my stomach on the floor beyond. I lay panting on the ground, panic subsiding as I chanced a glance at the walls and didn't see a single bone.

Pounding footsteps came from behind me.

I cursed under my breath as I suddenly remembered I was an asshat who had abandoned his friends.

"Elizabeth," I panted as I shakily pushed myself to my feet. "Elizabeth, I'm sorry."

Two figures moved out of the faint shadows by the arch.

"Elizabeth, run!" I shouted a second too late. The others had all sprinted through the archway, their faces a mix of anger, fear, and, in Devon's case, vague amusement.

"Behind you!" I pointed to the shadows as the arch crumbled, leaving a solid wall in its place.

"How exciting," Eric said, stepping in front of Elizabeth and Devon as the shadows began to take shape.

Longs fingers formed and disappeared. Dark fog swirled around their legs, like skirts blowing in the breeze.

It was...beautiful. Calm. I'd seen monsters come out of the shadows before, and there had always been a sense of evil oozing out of them. But these shadows seemed peaceful and kind. Which of course made me panic again.

"Eric, what's happening?" Elizabeth asked as proper hands and feet formed out of the shadows.

"I'm afraid to say I really haven't a clue."

A face formed. Wrinkled, worn, and smiling. Dark hair streaked with gray swirled into being.

Then two black women stood, smiling judgmentally at us.

"After all that work he just finds his way down here anyway." The first woman shook her finger at me.

"On the plus side, he made it here without getting himself killed," the second said.

"I don't know if I would call that a plus or a sign of being extra stupid," the first retorted.

"What?" I sputtered. I had been prepared to be attacked but not verbally.

"If you'll allow me to introduce myself." Eric stepped forward and gave a little bow, head to toe the pretentious douche I had met two months before. Not that I thought he had ever really changed, just maybe loosened up around us.

"Eric Deldridge." The first woman gave a bow. "Wizard, adventurer, fighter, who has escaped coming into our walls more times than I can count."

Eric bowed again, giving no sign he was flustered at someone keeping tabs on his near death experiences. "Quite right. Though I am afraid you have me at a disadvantage as I have no idea who you are."

"We are the ones they don't speak of," the second lady said. Now that my initial shock was over it was easy to tell she was younger than the first. Her hair only had tiny traces of gray.

"That would explain us not knowing who you are," Devon said.

Both of the women looked toward him.

"And this one doesn't belong to us," the older woman said. She dipped her head and studied Devon from the ground up. The warm glow of the light that seemed to come from nowhere, because why not, reflected off the white streaks in her hair.

"Strange we should know the name of one whose bones we shall never carry," the younger woman said. "But as I live and breathe, Devon Rhodes has broken into the Library and taken a stroll through the Vault of the Dead."

"I think I like *catacombs* better," I muttered.

"And dear, sweet Elizabeth Wick." The older lady stepped forward, arms outstretched toward Elizabeth. "Such a dear, sweet, brave girl."

"Don't touch her!" I yelped as the woman took Elizabeth's hand.

"You run through the dark looking for shadows, trying to find a way to help." The woman touched Elizabeth's cheek. "I'm sorry if my shadow added to your fear."

"I'm sorry," I said loudly enough that everyone turned to look at me, "but you know all of us, and apparently you've been scaring my girlfriend. So, I really need to know exactly who you are."

"Oh young love." The older woman laughed. "It's been such a long time, I hardly remember what it feels like."

"Something between sunshine and stupid as I recall." The younger woman laughed.

"I have seen you before," Elizabeth said. I couldn't tell if she was afraid or in awe. "I've seen you all over the city."

"We had to keep an eye on you, child." The older woman smiled. "When we find one like you, it becomes our happy obligation."

"And who are you that keeping an eye on young seers and hiding in dark corners is a part of your duties?" Eric asked like he was asking what borough they were from.

"We are the guardians of the dead." The younger woman spread her arms wide. "You have passed through our gates, and we welcome you to eternity."

My heart clenched in my chest, and both women burst out laughing.

"Don't scare the boy so." The older woman chuckled. "We have spent too much time trying to protect this one to scare him to death on our doorstep."

She looked into my eyes as she spoke, and they weren't filled with the terrifying void of a dark eternity. Their brown depths were caring and warm. Deep wrinkles formed around her eyes as she smiled at me, like centuries of laughter had carved themselves on her face.

"We are the ones who guard the dead. We are the seekers and buriers of the bones. We are two of the sisters who have been ordained to search the world for our deceased charges and given the honor of protecting them in death."

"But we're not dead," I said in a tone I hoped wasn't insulting. "So, why do you know us?"

"You follow a sweet boy for years making sure he doesn't get himself killed, and he doesn't even notice you," the older woman said.

"Typical," the younger added.

25

————

"You've been following me?" I squeaked.

"Not all the time. We have too much to do," the older woman said. "And it hasn't been just the two of us either. The Vault of the Dead can't be left unattended. We rotate *keep the child alive* duty."

"Why have you been following him?" Elizabeth stepped away from the women, taking my hand in hers.

Devon moved back too, blocking the women's path to me.

"Merlin's shiny bones, there's no need to protect the boy from us." The older woman tipped her head back and laughed.

I flinched as the sound ricocheted off the stone walls.

"You know about fate?" the older woman asked.

I nodded.

"The golden strands that bind all things together. That twist and pull and alter the way the world works based on her sorry whim?"

"Yeah," I said, hating myself for sounding like a kindergartener on the first day of school. "Yes, Eric's told me about fate."

"And Lola, too, no doubt." The younger woman nodded.

Eric's neck stiffened. "You know so much about us, might we at least know your names?"

"We gave up our names a long time ago. I won't insult the girl I used to be by dragging her into this dark place." The older woman didn't even bother looking at Eric. Her gaze stayed fixed on me. "If you know about fate, you know some people are wound up tight in the web, caught in so many different strings that to pull them away would leave a hole right in the middle of the pattern."

"Some holes are meant to be torn," the younger woman said. "Like a fire burning through the forest, you've got to clear out the old lives to make room for the new."

"But there are some folks"—the older woman raised a finger, pointing at my nose—"who are right in the middle of things. Who are needed for fate to push the world forward."

"And some of those people don't have the sense God gave peanuts and can't seem to keep themselves alive," the younger said.

"It has been a monumental amount of work trying to keep the web of fate intact when you keep trying to yank yourself out of it by dying. We have spent the last fourteen years keeping you alive." The older woman spoke the last word like a threat.

"Only fourteen?" Devon asked, a hint of humor in his tone.

"That was the first time he tried to wander out into traffic." The older woman gave a pinched smile and shook her head at Devon. "Tore his hand away from his mother and chased a puppy down the street."

"Good lord, that puppy wasn't even cute," the younger *tsked*. "Some stringy-looking nasty thing."

"I'm not even a dog person," I murmured. My brain couldn't move past the dog to people following me around trying to keep me alive. "I like cats."

"*I like cats.*" The older laughed. "That's why we've had so many problems with him."

"I've guessed it before," I said. Devon, Elizabeth, and Eric all looked at me. "I mean, not really like *Hey, there's crypt keepers saving my life.*"

"Crypt keepers?" the younger scoffed.

"But I sort of thought there might be a league of older black women trying to keep me alive…" I felt stupid and horrible for saying it.

But it was true. I couldn't count the number of times some old black lady had grabbed me by the hoodie and yanked me back before I could daydream my way into traffic. Or stared at me judgmentally enough that I stopped whatever stupid thing I was doing. Or asked why my backpack was screeching like I had a demonic mutant squirrel in it.

"You really have been following me." Somehow the revelation didn't feel creepy.

"I think there might be hope yet," the older said.

"But why?" Elizabeth asked. The women turned cold eyes on her, and she added hastily, "Not that I'm ungrateful for you keeping my boyfriend alive."

A thrill ran up my spine as she called me her boyfriend. Even while facing my judgmental, crypt keeper fairy godmothers, she still wanted to claim me.

"But why would you? Out of all the people in New York, or all the wizards even, why would you help Bryant?" Elizabeth finished.

"A very good question," Eric said.

"Thanks, guys," I grumbled.

"It is not our place to riddle out fate. We are only given glimpses of her plan," the older said, her voice more serious than it had been. "We see darkness, and we see light. The future can go either way. One push, and it could all tumble down."

"So Bryant's the guy standing on the middle of the magical good-and-evil teeter-totter?" Devon asked.

"How poetic," the younger said. "And yes, the fate of this one gangly boy reaches further into the golden strands than even we can see."

"You're seers?" Elizabeth asked.

I couldn't really blame her for skipping over my straddling good and evil. As far as I knew, Elizabeth had only ever met one other seer before.

"And witches," the older answered. "You have only one gift."

"One feels like a lot," Elizabeth said.

"How did you end up down here?" Devon asked. "This isn't like a seer retirement home, is it?"

"He thinks we're retired!" the older cackled.

"Another very good question, though," Eric said, stepping toward the women, his spine totally straight, looking regal in his suspicion. "I didn't think the Ladies would want other women running around their Library."

"We haven't seen the books in ages," the younger said, a hint of something nasty in her voice.

"Don't blame the child," the older said. "We've known for a long time how short the memories of those topside can be."

"Topside? Like not dead?" I gulped.

The women ignored me and pushed on.

"More than a century before your time, magic was dangerous for women," the older began. "Even more dangerous for women of color. The Ladies took control of the Library. They seized a way for women to shape the future of magic in Manhattan. It was a beautiful thing to behold."

"When they decided to bring all magical kin to a safe resting place, they knew they needed guards. Keepers of the dead who could travel out into the world to collect the bones of those who needed protection," the younger said. "They didn't want men.

Men would want to steal their power. Men would want to make their place under the Library greater than the Library itself. And that could never be allowed."

The older stepped forward. "We were a ready workforce. Trained to follow orders, happy to have a safe place to call our own. The Ladies named us the keepers of the dead."

"Wait," I said, accidentally cutting the younger off as she opened her mouth to speak. "Are you the originals? Have you been living underground for a century?"

"Let's just say we don't begrudge our trips topside to keep you from dying." The older woman smiled. "It gives us a nice chance for fresh air."

"But if you work for the Ladies, haven't you been going against them in keeping Bryant alive?" Elizabeth asked. "Again, not that I'm not grateful," she added sheepishly.

"The Ladies do not own us, nor do we work for them." The older woman spoke sternly. "We work for the dead. We assist fate to protect the future and keep the vault from filling before its time. But if the Ladies wanted to kill Bryant, we would not interfere."

"Death in battle wouldn't be an accident or even a misstep on the part of a foolish boy."

My face flushed hot.

"It would be the will of fate," the younger woman continued. "And we do not try and cheat fate."

"We hold too many within our walls who have been foolish enough to try just that." The older shook her head solemnly.

"Well then," Eric said, a little more brightly than the situation seemed to call for. "Let us hope fate holds favor with us today. Though it is good to know our bones will someday rest in such capable hands."

"You're welcome." The older bowed.

"We should be going." Eric turned to all of us. "There is much to be done."

"But I'm standing on a teeter-totter of doom! I want to know more about the teeter-totter and the knot of threads that..."

The older woman shook her head at me. "There are some things best not to know. Has it ever occurred to you that knowing too much of the future would only make it harder to keep walking toward it?"

"So it's bad?" My stomach seized up like all the strings fate had to offer had tangled themselves around my intestines.

Now the younger woman shook her head. "You just worry about keeping yourself alive. Fate's planned picture is bigger than you need to be worrying about."

"And don't trip over a book and die in the Library," the older said. "We can't follow you in there. Now go on. A whole lot of tomorrows are waiting on today."

"Tomorrows for me?" I asked.

"Go on." The older flapped her hands at me, shooing me down the hall.

"Okay, okay." Leaving my seer godmothers behind felt awkward. I wanted to hug them or ask for their address to send them a thank-you pie. I settled for "Thanks for keeping me alive."

"Try not to waste our hard work," the younger said, raising an eyebrow at Eric's back.

"Any advice?" Devon asked. "On, you know, surviving?"

"Turn back the way you came and find a nice quiet place to live out your years far away from here," the older said without a hint of sarcasm in her voice.

"I'll keep that in mind." Devon nodded.

"Till we meet again." Eric turned and gave one final bow.

"May it be years from now," the older woman said.

"See you around?" I asked.

The younger laughed dryly. "Try not to make us work too hard."

Elizabeth took my hand and led me down the hall. The back of my neck prickled familiarly. I could feel them watching. It wasn't quite as weird a feeling as it had been before.

"You okay, Bry?" Devon whispered.

"Just found out the keepers of the dead have been keeping me alive because I'm at the center of a knot in the web of fate that could tip the balance between good and evil." I shrugged. "It could be worse. At least there are no skulls here."

The corridor we traveled down was definitely nicer than the ones packed with bones. The warm glow hanging in the air made the stone walls seem pretty if not friendly.

"I still can't get used to it," Devon said after we'd been walking in silence for a few minutes.

I knew him well enough not to ask what *it* was.

He chewed his lip for a while before talking again. "The whole magical fate thing. That there's an invisible web that pulls us all around. And has you hogtied. It feels...prickly. Like I can feel it on my skin."

"You've spent enough time around magic, I wouldn't be surprised if you are actually starting to feel it." Eric stopped and looked at Devon appraisingly. "Perhaps magic will become your second language."

"Thanks?" Devon said to Eric's back as he kept walking, then mouthed to me, "What does that mean?"

The walls around us were hypnotizing. Not smooth and not covered with sharp ridges, but instead carved in gentle curves, like someone had lovingly scooped away the rock one minuscule spoonful at a time. Ahead, a branch in the tunnel came into view, one side sloping up, the other down.

"What's the plan?" I reverted back to whispering. The divergence of the hall suddenly made it real again. We were here to fight the Ladies.

"The upper path would be my best guess for getting into the main Library." Eric didn't stop walking forward. He didn't even slow down.

"Okay, so we take the upper path and then what?" I whispered. "How do we drive the Ladies out? Are we going to pen them in? Are we going to surprise them by charging the wrong way into The Consortium?"

"Perhaps" was Eric's only answer.

"Eric." I grabbed his arm, making him stop freakin' walking. "What are we going to do? What is the plan?"

"There is no plan," Eric said. "Quite frankly, I didn't think we'd make it this far."

"What?" Devon said.

"And I've never been in the Library," Eric pressed on. "I've never even seen a map of the Library. Obviously if I had, I would have known the Vault of the Dead was here. I can't formulate a plan without knowing what is ahead. I don't know why you would expect me to."

"Because you're the leader! You're the one who's supposed to know what to do!" I whisper-shouted at him.

"Well, I'm sorry to disappoint." Eric extricated his arm from my grasp. "But I'm nothing more than a wizard trying to leave this world a little bit less of a wreck than I found it." He straightened his bow tie. "And if I can have an adventure or two along the way, so much the better."

"Okay." Elizabeth stepped between Eric and me. "So we don't have a grand plan. Let's start small. What are we doing right now?"

"We're going up that hall and looking around," Devon answered. "We're going to see what's up there. We're going to keep quiet, scout the area, and find out if the Ladies are here. Then we come up with a plan."

He sounded so brave, so confident, I had to fight the urge to cheer.

"And what if the Ladies find us before we find them?" Elizabeth narrowed her sparkly eyes at Devon.

"We fight like hell and hope no one dies."

26

S talking through secret tunnels on your way to a forbidden Library can be kind of fun and exciting. But a few minutes into the upper tunnel and the deadliness of it all crept back into the adventure, and my palms slicked with sweat. After the third time I wiped my sweaty hands on my pants, a set of wide, polished double doors came into view.

"We shouldn't knock, right?" I whispered as we reached the doors. Shining brass handles stood out against the deep chocolate color of the wood. They towered over us, at least twelve feet high, looking more like they belonged in a mansion than in an underground stone tunnel.

"After me, I think." Eric stepped forward and took the handle.

I held my breath, waiting for the door to grow teeth and bite Eric in half, or to shock him and send him flying down the hall. But the handle just turned. Smoothly and quietly, as though the door saw regular use.

Giving us a nod, Eric swung the door slowly open. Standing on my tiptoes, I peered over his shoulder, waiting for spells to start flying.

Eric gasped, and *abalata* balanced on my lips as I waited to begin the fight. But Eric stepped forward, and I gasped, too.

We were at the bottom of a long spiral, which towered high above us. The space was wide enough for a few school buses to do donuts in. The walls around us bore carved white marble busts of women's faces. I recognized the one nearest us. She had been killed at the battle of Beville. I wanted to search the stone faces for the Ladies who were still alive and out for our blood, but I couldn't pull my gaze away from the ceiling high above.

Each tier of the spiral was more than twenty feet high, and at the top of the fifth level a beautiful mural of the night sky covered the ceiling. The stars weren't painted with normal gold paint. They were glittering as though someone had ripped stardust from the sky and trapped it in the picture.

A shining wooden banister wound its way down the five stories, and right beyond the rail, shelves peeked into view.

"It's massive," Devon whispered.

"It's beautiful," Elizabeth murmured.

"It's...it's..." I couldn't think of anything to add.

Eric said it for me. "It's magic."

I wanted to whoop, charge up the stairs, grab a book, and start finding out what I, Bryant Jameson Adams teen wizard, was really capable of. If it hadn't been for Devon taking my shoulder as I took the first step toward the tightly spiraled stairs that led to the next level up, I might have.

"They could be right up there," Devon whispered.

The edges of the shelves were visible, but, magic or not, it would be easy for a person to stay low and peer at us through the rails. The utter joy of it all drifted away, replaced by the horrible feeling of being watched.

Eric took the lead once again, keeping near the stone busts that lined the walls. Even the statues seemed to be glaring at me.

A horrible fleeting vision of cameras implanted in their eyeballs sent a shiver through my spine.

The steps in the spiral staircase were made of metal set in an intricate swirling design. The swooping curls had been worn away in places. How many times had the Ladies climbed these steps for their feet to wear away that much metal? How many thousands of books had the Ladies carried with them?

I crept up the stairs, trying not to let the metal *thunk* with my weight. My fingers buzzed with anticipation, itching to hold just one of the books. I'd read through most of Eric's volumes on magic, but these were new, forbidden.

At the top of the stairs I closed my eyes for a moment, preparing for the breathtaking beauty of knowledge I was about to behold.

"No." Eric's horrified whisper tore me away from my beatific anticipation.

My eyes sprang open, ready for death to rain on us from above. But Eric was just standing there, staring at the floor-to-ceiling shelves, his face pale and vaguely ill looking.

"What's..." My voice faded away as I looked at the shelves, made of beautiful shining wood that gleamed in the light, with delicate scrollwork carved around the edges. They were utterly empty.

"No," Eric murmured again, as if refusing to accept reality could somehow change it. "No!" He took off running the circle of the layer. I charged after him, my heart pounding in my chest. I glanced over my shoulder just long enough to be sure Devon and Elizabeth were following before looking back to the shelves.

They were *all* empty. Perfectly dusted, wood unscratched, and totally empty.

Eric charged up the steps to the next level before I could catch him. I tore up the stairs, praying the next level would be filled with books, but the shelves were bare.

"Eric!" I hissed as he sprinted the circumference of the next level. "Eric, come back!"

He didn't listen, so we all just kept running after him, passing shelf after empty shelf. I tried not to do the math. How many books missing from how many shelves?

Thousands. Just on one level. Thousands and thousands of one-of-a-kind books. Centuries of irreplaceable knowledge.

"Eric, stop!"

He ran up to the next level, his footfalls clanging on the metal steps.

The Ladies were going to hear him. Any second they would come charging out to kill us. But there was no way to stop Eric without making even more noise as he circled the third floor and up the steps to the forth.

I was in way better shape than I had been the first time I had run with Eric, but he was still faster than the rest of us. I was barely up the steps to the fourth floor when he clambered up the stairs to the fifth.

"Eric!" I panted completely in vain. Tears burned in the corners of my eyes. I don't know if it was because we had done so much to get to the books and they weren't here, or if I was terrified of what the Ladies might have done to them.

At the top of the last flight of stairs, the view was different. The ceiling reflected a shimmering pattern of stars on everything around us. It should have been breathtaking. Half the circle was covered with shelves, but the other half was taken up by three large doorways. Eric knelt in front of one, his head in his hands.

I ran over to him, searching the other doors for signs of evil, killer-mist Ladies.

The door Eric had collapsed in front of was covered in bars like an old-fashioned bank vault or jail cell. I held my breath, hoping there wouldn't be more skeletons hidden in there.

There were no white bones in the locked room. Nothing that even resembled people. The space was as big as my mom's linoleum-floored apartment, and the walls had been scorched black by fire. Scattered around the room, under chunks of burned shelves and the blackened remains of a single chair, were the singed remnants of books.

"Why?" Eric whispered. "How?"

"We have to keep moving." Devon reached down to Eric.

"Everything." Eric sounded like his best friend had been burned in the room with the books. "Everything for centuries, gone."

"We don't know that." Devon seized Eric's arm and dragged him to his feet. "All we know is the shelves are empty. That doesn't change what we came here to do. We have to drive the Ladies out, and if we get a chance to question them along the way, all the better."

Eric swayed. "Records from around the world. Scrolls and papyrus."

"Eric." Devon took Eric's face in his hands. "We will find out what happened to the books. I promise we will do whatever it takes to find them. But we have to keep moving before the Ladies find us."

"Too late," Elizabeth said, her words shockingly loud as they resonated off the ceiling.

I spun to face her, expecting to see a knife at her throat, but she stood alone, pointing at the farthest door where three Ladies waited, mist lapping at their feet.

27

Tendrils of cold tore at my skin. Elizabeth, Devon, and I froze, staring. The childish idea that if you don't move they can't see you seemed to have taken over all our instincts.

"Where are they?" Eric growled.

His perfect hair spiked out of place. His eyes gleamed wildly. He was a man filled with grief and rage and was more terrifying than I had ever seen him.

"Where are the books?" Eric spat, stepping in front of the three of us. "What have you done with them?"

"The intruders came to steal our books," the oldest of the Ladies said. Even from a distance, her overly wrinkled skin seemed paper thin and crackly. "And now they can't find them."

"They'll just have to die without seeing the precious books," the second Lady said, a savage joy filling her voice as it bounced off the ceiling and echoed around the landing. "Our books cannot be stolen."

"We haven't come to steal anything." I felt my lips form the words, so I knew it had to be me speaking.

"Then why would they come?" the last Lady said, her voice higher than the other two. Like she was barely a teenager trapped in the pure white form of the Ladies. "Why would they come to die if they have nothing to gain?"

"We seek to gain nothing," Eric said, his voice so low it was more frightening than if he had been screaming. "We've come to take everything from you. *Erunca!*"

Three bolts of lightning streaked down from the star mural like Zeus himself had thrown them. With a *hiss*, the Ladies scattered, dodging Eric's spell.

"I will cast you out of your power." Eric stalked toward the Ladies, magic crackling around him. "*Enestoliot.*" Lightning formed in Eric's hands, surrounding his fists before he threw it at the nearest Lady.

Mist formed in front of her, eating the power of Eric's spell, lighting the cloud from within.

"Kill them all," the wrinkled Lady said the moment before she charged Eric.

The high-voiced Lady launched herself over the railing, and for a moment I thought she would fall, but a wind rose around her, carrying her straight toward Devon.

"Oh, of course the young one is attracted to me," Devon laughed, pulling his sword from his pocket.

"*Primurgo!*" I shouted, blocking the Lady from Devon, but I couldn't wait to see if the spell had done any good because the last Lady had come for me, sweeping along the railing like a misty-white bat.

"*Abalata!*" I screamed, throwing the black from my hand as soon as it formed. It found its mark, hitting the Lady square in the stomach. She doubled over for a second, just long enough for me to watch Elizabeth scream, "This way, you old hag!" from the doorway where the Ladies had appeared. She took off down the hall, the wrinkled Lady swooping after her in a rage, Eric chasing them, bellowing a spell that streaked red through the air.

That moment of worrying about why my girlfriend was trying to get herself killed was too much. The Lady I was facing had pulled herself upright and hovered six inches above the ground, glaring at me.

"*Telinto*," the woman said casually.

A white-hot something slashed my face, spraying my blood across the marble floor.

"*Kunga!*" I shouted.

The woman flew back, hitting the rail.

I waited for her to take a step forward. "*Turso!*" The spell knocked her feet out from under her but not in the direction I had intended. Instead of falling face first on the floor she tipped backward over the railing.

"No!" I screamed as she fell out of sight. But there was nothing I could do. I spun to Devon, who looked like he was dancing with the Lady he fought.

She giggled wildly like they were playing a game. Grasping a sword of mist made solid, she beamed with joy while she dueled Devon. I ran toward the fight. If the Lady got tired of playing games with him, she could slaughter him with a whisper.

Devon parried her blow just like he'd done to Tybalt in *Romeo and Juliet* two years ago and shouted, "Go after yours, Bry. Finish it!"

The Lady lunged forward, and Devon arched his torso to the side, barely missing being sliced by her blade. "Is that the best you've got?" Devon laughed.

I didn't know what the right thing to do was, but my feet carried me to the bannister in two long strides, and I vaulted over the wooden rail. "*Escata*." I kept my eyes on the floor far below as I fell, spotting the Lady as the feeling of landing in pudding began.

Bright red blood dripped from her head, staining her otherwise perfect whiteness. She opened her mouth, but I was a split second faster.

"*Aarantha!*" A whirlwind formed around me, pressing the Lady back into the wall. Mist pulled from her like yarn unraveling from a blanket.

Through the roar of the wind I heard a muffled shout. Pain shot through my arm as a deep gash appeared.

"*Erunca!*" Streaks of lightning swirled though the vortex in jarring strips.

The Lady screamed in agony the instant before a cut appeared right over my heart.

I coughed at the pain, wanting nothing more than to press my hands to wound, but I couldn't let go of my spell.

The Lady's eyes peered through the wind, glowing with hate and brimming with joy. She wouldn't stop until she killed me.

"*Caruson!*" I bellowed, hoping my half-formed plan would work. A round of crashes circled the room as each of the marble busts broke free from their bases. The stone heads caught in the twister, flying toward the living Lady.

With a cackle she batted one out of my storm, sending it flying toward my head.

Throwing myself to the ground, I dodged the marble missile. A second head exploded two inches from my own. The voice inside me that believes things work out in the end for good people told me to duck again. To try a spell to pin the Lady to the wall until Eric could find a way to lock her in the burned vault.

Then I pushed myself back to my feet, and my eyes landed on the bright red streak of my own blood smeared across on the floor. The Lady was going to kill me. And then she would move on to my friends.

"*Ilmatiot.*" Dread filled me as I said the spell. I had never used it before. I didn't know the surge that would fly through me as magic blasted from my body. I didn't expect the moment of hollowness once the spell reached the Lady. I didn't know how strong my panic would be as she gasped, fighting for the breath I squeezed from her body.

She clawed at her throat like she was trying to free the thing that was choking her, but that wasn't how the spell worked.

Thaden himself had used it on me. I knew all too well the horrible searing pain as her lungs fought to expand, the dizzying crash as she fell to the floor, the panic as she realized there was nothing she could do.

I didn't let go of the spell. I could've stopped it, could've let her breathe. But I didn't. I stood there in the center of the tornado I had created and watched her die.

She gave me one last hateful glare before her eyes went blank.

28

One more for the Vault of the Dead.

That was the sick thought in my head as I let go of the twister. My knees buckled, and I hit the marble floor.

I wanted to curl up and never move again. I probably would have, but Devon screamed high above, and I knew I had to keep going. Devon, Elizabeth, Eric—they were why I had to fight. They needed me, and I couldn't abandon them to wallow in fear.

"*Sinato,*" I said as I stumbled to the stairs. The sting of the spell healing my skin hurt almost as badly as the cutting itself.

Devon screamed again.

"Devon, hold on!" I shouted, running faster than I had in my entire life.

I caught a glimpse of him rolling away from a shattered piece of banister.

"Hold on, Devon," I whispered as I reached the fourth floor. "Just hold on."

A shriek of laughter from the Lady made my heart vault to my throat. But there were still sounds of fighting. Fighting meant alive.

"I'm here!" I shouted as I leapt the last few feet to the fifth floor.

"Good timing," Devon growled through clenched teeth. The Lady had him pinned to the wall, her mist sword pressing on his light saber in an attempt to force him to decapitate himself.

I stared at them for a moment. Devon poured sweat, his muscles shaking from the fight. Blood seeped from a cut on his neck, dripped from his hand, and covered his thigh. The Lady beamed like she was gleefully awaiting a ride on a Ferris wheel of death, her white untainted.

"Anytime, Bry," Devon grunted.

My mind raced, trying to find a spell that would stop her from decapitating my best friend without me accidentally decapitating my best friend. I had nothing.

Schoolyard instinct took over. I grabbed a piece of the broken banister and charged, screaming at the top of my lungs. My wordless battle cry shook the ceiling.

The Lady wasn't dumb enough to let go of Devon just because I was howling at her, so I raised the hunk of wood high and bashed her on the head with it, knocking her away from Devon.

I opened my mouth to start a trapping spell, but Devon got there first, plunging his sword into the Lady's chest. She didn't even scream before she went limp.

Gasping for breath, Devon pulled his sword free. There wasn't any blood. The heat of the blade had cauterized the wound. It was like she was meant to have an awkward burned hole in the middle of her chest.

"You okay?" Devon panted, tearing his eyes from the dead Lady. His eyes didn't have the crippling fear of having just killed someone that sloshed painfully around in my chest. He looked hollow.

"Fine." I swallowed. There wasn't time to worry about

emotional trauma or anything more than if either of us was about to bleed to death. "Let me help." I raised my hands to do a healing spell.

"There isn't time."

Ignoring him I muttered the spell and watched his skin shimmer as it healed the cut on his neck—which was too close to his jugular for comfort—the swiftly bleeding wound on his palm, and the gash across his thigh.

"We have to go." Devon ran to the door where Eric and Elizabeth had disappeared before his skin had finished knitting back together.

We ran quietly. I wanted to ask Devon what the plan was, but I knew what he would say. *Find Eric and Elizabeth, make sure they don't get killed, try to make sure we don't get killed either.*

The doorway they had taken led to a hall that looked... normal. Well, normal for my dad's super rich friends.

Evenly spaced chandeliers dripped from the ceiling, marble tables held vases of flowers, and paintings hung in gold leaf frames. The first painting was the size of a car and showed a man standing on top of a rock, summoning lightning from above. I wanted to stop and study it, to find out who the magical man was. But singe marks marred the fancy red wallpaper, and swatches of the patterned rug had been torn away. We ran on, the thickness of the tattered ground muffling our footfalls.

I kept listening, waiting for Elizabeth to scream. It's weird to hope someone will scream, but screaming means alive.

Devon grabbed my arm as we reached the double door at the end of the hall, yanking me back before I could wrench them open.

"Shhh." Devon leaned close to the doorjamb, pausing for a moment before opening the door a crack and listening again.

"Let's go," I whispered.

"Who's in a hurry now?" Devon pulled the door open far enough to peek into the next room. "Empty."

The square room was empty at least as far as people. Matching desks were laid out in a grid on the shining wooden floor. All of the desks had been cleared but three.

Only one now.

The thought shook me to my spine as we ran across the parquet floor, our shoes clacking. A door led out of each side of the room. All the doors were closed. Panic surged, gripping my lungs. There was no way to know which way they went, and no time to search.

"There." Devon pointed to a scorch mark above the left-hand door.

I charged toward the door, not even caring if it wasn't Eric being brilliant at all but a trap from the wrinkled Lady. I reached the door first and wrenched the knob, not giving Devon the time to listen. The girl of my dreams and the man who brought me into this world were fighting somewhere, and I had to reach them.

"How dare you!" The Lady's shriek of rage flew down the narrow corridor we'd just entered, echoing off the concrete walls.

My heart leapt. If she had someone to scream at, someone was still alive and fighting her.

The hall ended in a sharp corner, and lights flashed around the bend. I sprinted down the corridor, my feet barely touching the floor.

A crash of a spell striking something solid rattled toward us.

"*Ellisium!*" the Lady screamed.

"You are finished here!" Eric bellowed. "You are done. I will not allow you destroy one more ounce of magic."

As I rounded the corner, bright red light nearly blinded me

and I skidded to a stop. Shielding my eyes, I tried to understand the scene in front of me.

Elizabeth was on her feet, four limbs attached and breathing like a champ, next to Eric who had streams of red light pouring out of his palms. The Lady screamed, trapped inside a glowing scarlet cocoon, which had tipped her onto her back and pressed her toward the floor as though the spell held the force of gravity itself. Only the strength of her own magic kept her hovering a foot above the ground.

"Tell me where the books are," Eric growled.

"The books are not meant for men like you," the Lady spat. Even in the red light her skin shone white, making her look more like a corpse than a person capable of speech.

"Tell me where you've hidden them." The magic in Eric's hands redoubled, squeezing in around the Lady.

Her face twisted in rage and pain as she screamed. "You will never see those books, you foolish child."

"If I am a child to you, then know a child has taken your Library, a child has overthrown the Ladies, and a child will find where you've hidden the books." Eric's eyes danced in the light of his own magic, giving him the look of a madman rather than a wizard.

"The books have not been in these walls since you walked on this earth." Each word the Lady spoke seemed to cost her energy she didn't have. "The best of us have sought them and failed." A laugh like a scream flew from the Lady, echoing off the walls. "Die in the attempt, fool."

A *whoosh* of magic tore through the hall, knocking me over as it dove into Eric's spell.

And the last Lady went limp, falling to the floor in an undignified heap.

"No!" Eric bolted forward and grabbed the Lady, taking her by the shoulders and shaking her so hard she looked like a shriveled rag doll. "You don't get to be dead!" He began murmuring under his breath.

"Eric," Elizabeth said, her voice shaking.

Eric didn't look up. He held the Lady in his arms. She didn't look terrifying anymore. Just old and sad.

"Eric!" Elizabeth said loudly enough Eric couldn't ignore her. "Eric, she's dead."

The world froze for a moment. The enormity of the truth settled around us, falling heavily on my skin.

I know it sounds crazy, but for the first time, and only for a split second, it was like I could feel the strings of fate. Feel the golden strands that had surrounded the Ladies snap. The long line of women who had ruled magic for so long was gone, the last of them lay dead before me. My skin prickled like the threads were searching, finding a new life to latch on to, adding more weight to the web that already wrapped so tightly around my life.

And then the feeling was gone.

Eric let go of the Lady, and she fell back to the floor. "She had no right to die."

"That wasn't you?" Devon asked, sounding as tired as I felt.

"She did it to herself, to keep the books from me. From the people who deserve them." Eric cursed and banged his fists on the concrete wall. Shockwaves of magic flew from his hands, denting the surface.

"Where are the other two?" Elizabeth asked.

"Dead."

Elizabeth looked into my eyes as I said the word, and I knew she knew. She saw the horrible fear that had settled just above my spleen. She saw the panic in my eyes. I had killed a witch. A human. Not fought for my life and vaguely wondered later if my opponent had survived. Not incapacitated and let someone else make the final blow. Not killed a monster before it could squash my friends. I had watched the life leave the Lady's body, and I wasn't sure if I regretted it. Elizabeth didn't need to be a seer to see the burden death had laid on me.

"We did it." There was no triumph in Devon's voice. "We took the Library from the Ladies."

"It wasn't supposed to happen like this," Elizabeth said.

"No one was supposed to die." The word *die* tasted like bleach in my mouth.

"There were supposed to be books!" Eric buried his face in his hands.

"Eric." Devon laid his hand on Eric's shoulder. "We came here to take the Library from the Ladies. To make sure they weren't in power so they couldn't come after us for what happened in Beville. The Ladies are gone. They can't hurt us or anyone else ever again."

"But the books." Eric dragged his hands across his face so hard it looked like he'd tear his own skin off. "What good is the Library without the books? How can we tell the magical world the Ladies are gone and so are the centuries of magical learning we've been begging for all our lives?"

"The books haven't been here during your life," Elizabeth said. "The whole time you've been wanting them, the shelves have been empty."

"Can we not be here right now?" I asked. Having a conversation over a dead body was too much for me.

No one said anything, but Elizabeth took my hand and led me away. I didn't look back to make sure Devon and Eric were following us. I didn't want to see the body again.

"Why weren't there any mist monsters?" Devon asked when we reached the room with the desks and shut the hall door firmly behind us. "I'm not complaining, but why didn't we meet any of their nasty little friends?"

"Only the Ladies could be allowed in the presence of the books." Eric sounded numb as he spoke.

"And little killer mist pets didn't make it through the ban?" A laugh rose in my throat and died before it made a sound.

"They kept their secret from their minions though it cost them their lives," Eric said.

"Which way?" Elizabeth asked.

The temptation to curl up and sleep under one of the desks overwhelmed me. I didn't want to find a way out. I didn't want to go into the crisp winter air and see the world was still turning like I hadn't just killed someone.

But the world doesn't wait for you to be ready.

Numbly, I walked to one of the doors we hadn't been through. It led to a short hall lined with doors, sort of like the wing we slept in in Eric's house. Not bothering to close that door, I moved on to the last one and was greeted by a long staircase.

The steps weren't made of fancy metal. They were worn wood like we had accidentally stumbled into the basement of a brownstone.

"This way?" I asked. Not waiting for a response, I climbed the steps.

The first stair creaked and I started to shout a spell before realizing the step wasn't trying to attack me.

"What did Thaden take?" Eric asked as we trudged up the stairs. "He broke into the Library. He found the spells he put on the phone. If the books weren't here—"

"The burned room," Devon said. "My Lady said Thaden torched the last of the books in the vault. Said she'd burn me in there, too."

"He just burned them?" I hate to say that I hated Thaden, but I did. He tried to kill me, and it all sort of spiraled from there. Knowing he'd burned precious magical records tripled my loathing. I finally understood what it must have been like to find out the Great Library of Alexandria had been burned, and the feeling was nothing less than utterly sick.

"He recorded the knowledge in the phone for his own use and destroyed the rest," Eric said as the stairs finally came to an end. "I have never conceived of such depths of evil."

A door waited for us at the top of the stairs. Nothing strange or beautiful, just a door with a faint scent of food wafting through.

The door moved with one quick shove, and I knew where we were before Devon said, "The Consortium."

We had made it all the way back. Under the river, through Hell, and back to midtown. I didn't know whether to laugh or cry.

"I'll get food." Devon headed toward the swinging door in the back. Suddenly it seemed like a hundred years since we'd eaten the overpriced turkey sandwiches from the ferry.

"Is there anyone back there?" Elizabeth called after him.

Because that's how wonderful she was. Thinking of things like if there's henchmen making eggs.

"All clear," Devon called back.

Eric sagged into a chair, looking utterly defeated even though we'd just won.

"Thaden knew." Elizabeth slipped into the chair opposite Eric. "He must have seen the empty shelves. He knew there were no more books. Why didn't he tell everyone? Why did he bother fighting the Ladies at all? He could have just told everyone the books were missing, and the Ladies would have lost all their power over Beville. Over everyone."

"Missing?" Eric said. "Thousands of books don't just go missing. If the Ladies couldn't find them, they were stolen by someone very brave and extremely magically talented."

"How do you know they looked for them?" I asked. My brain

had gotten to the muddy phase where you can't quite understand the flow of your own thoughts, let alone anyone else's.

"*The best of us have sought them,*" Eric recited the Lady's
words. "They would only call themselves the best of anything. If
the Ladies were looking for the books, someone else took them."

"Who?" Elizabeth asked, wiping blood from the cuts on her
forearms. It looked like the Lady had clawed her.

Feeling like the worst boyfriend in the world, I murmured,
"*Sinato*" and held her hands as the spell knitted the skin back
together.

"Eric?" I asked after a long moment. "Who could have taken
the books?"

"A hundred unlikely people," Eric sighed. "And I haven't the
faintest clue as to where to find them."

"But I still don't understand why Thaden didn't tell everyone
the books were gone," Elizabeth said. "It would have wreaked
more havoc than anything else he could have done."

"If you found out a priceless treasure was missing, would
you tell everyone, or would you search while no one else knew
there was anything to even be searching for?" Devon said, laying
a chocolate cake and four forks on the table. "That kitchen is
shockingly bare." Devon shrugged when Eric raised a ques-
tioning eyebrow at him.

I grabbed a fork and tore free a bit of cake. "Do you think
Thaden found the books?"

"No," Eric said, sounding more himself after a bite of cake.
"If he had them, he would have told everyone. Thaden never
found the books."

"So now we have to find a way to do something Thaden
never managed?" Devon stabbed his fork into the cake a little
harder than necessary. "I might need coffee to go with this cake."

Eric froze looking at Devon. "You'll help me find the books?"

"We'll all help you find the books," Devon said. "And figure out a way to stop Kendrick McDonald from hunting Bryant and whatever other new blood he's after."

"That's a really big to-do list for only being two items long." I shoved a huge bite of cake into my mouth. I don't know if the Ladies had been excellent bakers, outsourced, or just magicked the cake into being, but it was moist perfection. The rush of sugar flowed through my veins, and suddenly trying to take down a wizard-trafficking ring and find a few thousand lost books seemed not entirely suicidal.

"Do we tell people the Ladies are dead?" Elizabeth asked with the most tantalizing crumb of cake on her lip.

"No," Eric said. "Having the Ladies be gone without having a new government in place would be chaos."

"Are we going to turn Elizabeth pasty and make her a fake Lady?" Devon asked.

"Are we going to bleach Devon and dress him in drag?" Elizabeth countered.

"Neither." Eric stood, ignoring Devon and Elizabeth staring each other down. "I happen to know a seer who has spent far too long living in exile. I think a change in address is just what she needs."

"So we grab Lola from under the bridge and make her the head of the magical world?" I asked.

"Yes." Eric's face lightened as he walked toward the window that looked out over the park and Big Blue in all its early morning glory.

"Then we stalk Kendrick McDonald and make sure he can't hurt anyone again?" Elizabeth led me to the window, wrapping her arm around my waist so she could lean into my shoulder.

"Precisely."

"Then we find the books and create free knowledge for magickind?" Devon joined the group.

"Exactly."

"And hope all of our parents will take us back and we're not expelled from school?" Devon added.

"I have plenty of spare room in Beville." Eric smiled. "And I hear The Consortium might need a new busboy besides."

Devon glared at Eric.

"All the best magical restaurants have busboys with swords." Eric bowed.

"I want a magical shield," Devon said. "Maybe a suit of armor, too."

Devon started to laugh, and then we were all laughing, because there was nothing else to do.

We stood together in the window of The Consortium, watching the Christmas tourists pass. None of them knew there was no line for a table at The Consortium. None of them knew we had all almost died. And none of them knew we had all just agreed to take on most of the magical world to save magickind. Whether they liked it or not.

Bryant, Elizabeth, and the gang will return. In order to stay up to date on the latest releases from Megan O'Russell, be sure to sign up for her readers community at https://meganorussell.com/book-signup.

A DARKER TASTE

Two worlds. One glass wall. No turning back.

The human race has been divided. The chosen few live in the safety of the domes, watching through their glass walls as those left on the outside suffer and die. But desperation has brought invention. New drugs have the ability to alter humans, giving them the strength to roam the poisoned night unafraid—but survival comes at a terrible price.

Seventeen-year-old Nola Kent has spent her life in the domes, training to protect her little piece of the world within the glass. The mission of the domes is to preserve the human race, not to help the sick and starving.

When the fate of an outsider child falls into her hands, Nola dares to venture beyond the security of her home, diving into a world of darkness and vampires. Life within the glass didn't prepare her for the realities of suffering or the depth of forbidden love.

When blood washes over the domes, Nola must choose between her home and her heart.

Read on for a sneak preview.

CHAPTER ONE

Nola dug her fingers into the warm dirt. Around her, the greenhouse smelled of damp earth, mist, and fresh, clean air.

Carefully, she took the tiny seed and placed it at the bottom of the hole her finger had made.

Thump.

Soon the seed would take root. A sprout would break through to the surface.

Thump, bang.

Then the green stem would grow until bean pods sprouted.

Bang, thump!

The food would be harvested and brought to their tables. All of the families would be fed.

"Ahhhhh!" the voice came from the other side of the glass. Nola knew she shouldn't look, but she couldn't ignore the sounds any longer.

It was a woman this time, her skin gray with angry, red patches dotting her face. She slammed her fists into the glass, leaving smears of red behind. The woman didn't seem to care as she banged her bloody hands into the glass over and over.

"Magnolia."

Nola jumped as Mrs. Pearson placed a hand on her shoulder.

"Don't pay her any mind," Mrs. Pearson said. "She can't get through the glass."

"But she's bleeding." Nola pushed the words past the knot in her throat.

The woman bashed her head against the glass.

"She needs help," Nola said. The woman stared right at her.

Mrs. Pearson took Nola's shoulders and turned her back to her plant tray. "That woman is beyond your help, Magnolia. Paying her any attention will only make it worse. There is nothing you can do."

Nola felt eyes staring at her. Not just the woman on the other side of the glass. The rest of the class was staring at her now, too.

Bang. Thump.

Families. The food she planted would feed the families.

Bang.

Pop.

Nola spun back to the glass. Two guards were outside now. One held his gun high. A thin spike protruded from the woman's neck. Her eyelids fluttered for a moment before she slid down the glass, leaving a streak of blood behind her.

"See," Mrs. Pearson said, smoothing Nola's hair, "they'll take her where she can't hurt herself or any of us ever again."

Nola nodded, turning back to the tray of dirt. Make a hole, plant the seed, grow the food. But the streaks of blood were burned into her mind.

Free to Read from Your Favorite Online Retailer

ESCAPE INTO ADVENTURE

Thank you for reading Seven Things Not to Do When Everyone's Trying to Kill You. If you enjoyed the book, please consider leaving a review to help other readers find Bryant's story.

As always, thanks for reading,

Megan O'Russell

Never miss a moment of the danger or hilarity.

Join the Megan O'Russell mailing list to stay up to date on all the action by visiting https://www.meganorussell.com/book-signup.

ABOUT THE AUTHOR

Megan O'Russell is the author of several Young Adult series that invite readers to escape into worlds of adventure. From *Girl of Glass*, which blends dystopian darkness with the heart-pounding danger of vampires, to *Ena of Ilbrea*, which draws readers into an epic world of magic and assassins.

With the *Girl of Glass* series, *The Tethering* series, *The Chronicles of Maggie Trent*, *The Tale of Bryant Adams,* the *Ena of Ilbrea* series, and several more projects planned for 2020, there are always exciting new books on the horizon. To be the first to hear about new releases, free short stories, and giveaways, sign up for Megan's newsletter by visiting the following:

https://www.meganorussell.com/book-signup.

Originally from Upstate New York, Megan is a professional musical theatre performer whose work has taken her across North America. Her chronic wanderlust has led her from Alaska to Thailand and many places in between. Wanting to travel has fostered Megan's love of books that allow her to visit countless new worlds from her favorite reading nook. Megan is also a lyricist and playwright. Information on her theatrical works can be found at RussellCompositions.com.

She would be thrilled to chat with you on Facebook or Twitter @MeganORussell, elated if you'd visit her website MeganORussell.com, and over the moon if you'd like the pictures of her adventures on Instagram @ORussellMegan.

ALSO BY MEGAN O'RUSSELL

The Girl of Glass Series

Girl of Glass

Boy of Blood

Night of Never

Son of Sun

The Tale of Bryant Adams

How I Magically Messed Up My Life in Four Freakin' Days

Seven Things Not to Do When Everyone's Trying to Kill You

The Tethering Series

The Tethering

The Siren's Realm

The Dragon Unbound

The Blood Heir

The Chronicles of Maggie Trent

The Girl Without Magic

The Girl Locked With Gold

The Girl Cloaked in Shadow

Ena of Ilbrea

Wrath and Wing

Ember and Stone

Mountain and Ash

Feather and Flame

Made in the USA
San Bernardino, CA
06 May 2020